after the death of Alice Bennett

Rowland Molony

OXFORD
UNIVERSITY PRESS

OXFORD
UNIVERSITY PRESS

Great Clarendon Street, Oxford OX2 6DP

Oxford University Press is a department of the University of Oxford.
It furthers the University's objective of excellence in research, scholarship,
and education by publishing worldwide in

Oxford New York

Auckland Cape Town Dar es Salaam Hong Kong Karachi
Kuala Lumpur Madrid Melbourne Mexico City Nairobi
New Delhi Shanghai Taipei Toronto

With offices in

Argentina Austria Brazil Chile Czech Republic France Greece
Guatemala Hungary Italy Japan Poland Portugal Singapore
South Korea Switzerland Thailand Turkey Ukraine Vietnam

Oxford is a registered trade mark of Oxford University Press
in the UK and in certain other countries

British Library Cataloguing in Publication Data
Data available

ISBN-13: 978-0-19-275472-1

3 5 7 9 10 8 6 4 2

Typeset by Newgen Imaging Systems (P) Ltd., Chennai, India
Printed in Great Britain by
Cox & Wyman Ltd, Reading, Berkshire

Paper used in the production of this book is a natural,
recyclable product made from wood grown in sustainable forests.
The manufacturing process conforms to the environmental
regulations of the country of origin.

. . . it is the rule that the land of the dead observes icy silence, unperturbed by the grief of the bereaved.

C.G. Jung

Acknowledgements

To Emma for perceptive commentaries and corrections, to Susie for an early conversation about the Next World's tardiness in the comms department, to Matt for a wonderful work space, to Wendy and Rob for keenness and for transporting the shed, to Janice for having initial faith, to Polly for a fuelling enthusiasm and the astute editing that has shaped this story, to Josephina for so generously giving translation advice, to Joyce for a tattooed Medium and a psychic lorry driver, to Sylvie for Alice, to everyone who is a part of St Luke's Hospice in Sheffield, to Suzy for lots of love, and to Elizabeth for love and patience: Thank you.

For Elizabeth

Chapter One

We've got mafia waiting outside the crematorium.

Sam repeated Becky's dry observation silently to himself. What? What did she mean?

He looked up at his sister, but she had buried her face in Dad's neck for a few moments. Her knuckles were white, gripping his arm.

'Hey . . . Hey. Hold on, lass,' Dad was saying. 'There . . . it's OK. We're nearly done here. Listen, Becky love, I've to talk to folk while they come out. You tek Sam over the way; have a sit down under the trees. We'll go home in a few minutes.'

Sam watched Becky and his dad clenched, holding on to each other. They had just come out of the chapel, the three of them, ahead of all the people. They had this moment, just this moment together. Then it was over and the double doors burst open behind them and people spilled out, a tide of people parting and flowing either side of them, pulling off jackets and loosening ties and dabbing at their eyes with tissues, all heading for the open doors and the sunlight.

Becky took his hand and drew him outside. Hot light blinded him.

'Becky, what did you mean? What's the mafia?'

1

She didn't answer. Head down, she hustled him past the young men in their charcoal suits and dark glasses who were standing around on the tarmac where the black hearse had swung round in a big circle, and walked them both onto the shaved lawns and under the shady trees. She pulled him down and they sat cross-legged on the grass under shifting spots of sunlight.

Sam watched her mend her face with tissues.

'Forget it, Sam. I was just getting irritable with some of the boys. See them standing around over there in their dark suits and shades? Just because they're at a funeral . . . ' She gave a half-laugh. 'And they were late, so none of them had the bottle to come in.' She stared over at the groups of people standing and talking in the sunshine. 'Mum would have laughed. She taught half of them when they were little boys.'

Sam too looked across to the entrance of the cremat-orium. So many people. Neighbours. Teachers from Mum's school. Men and women who worked at Dad and Uncle Roy's firm, *Bennett Brothers Agricultural Contractors and Hauliers*. And the teenage boys in their black suits and dark glasses.

'I know him . . . and I know him, and . . . him.' Sam picked them off.

'Of course you do. Some of them have been to our house. They're my friends in the Sixth Form.'

Sam watched his dad greeting people as they came down the steps, squinting in the sun. Mr Mack came out, wiping his forehead with a white hanky. And Mrs Prythurch who lived two doors down the road and whose husband had died a few months back. Auntie Pam came down the steps shining in pink and white among all the dull grey clothes, the dark suits.

Becky had slipped dark glasses on and was checking her mobile phone for messages. And there was a message because the silver pod gave out a small double-chime.

Sam blinked in the bright light and noted that he was dry-eyed. Ought he to be crying? He didn't feel like crying. There had been moments in the service when he had felt a kind of dissolving behind his eyes, when different people had come up to the front to read poems or tell little stories about Mum, and when they said things that brought her back to life. They had described her, and he had seen her so clearly in those moments. Like when she laughed with her eyes creased and her head thrown back, her throat exposed, or when she talked over her shoulder into the back of the car without taking her eyes off the road, or when she walked up the stairs carrying a pile of ironed clothes. He didn't feel like crying now. But he felt all pushed-up into the very front of his head; there was something gathered behind his eyes, something waiting.

He had some thinking to do. About all this. And Mum.

Once or twice in the chapel he had allowed a picture in his head: Mum lying on her back inside the long box with the shining handles. Just for a second, then he thought of something else. That wouldn't be his mum. How could she . . . ?

He looked at the Order of Service which was still in his hands, rolled into a tube. He opened it out: *Celebrating the Life of Alice Bennett*. It listed the names of all the people who had walked up to the front of the chapel and spoken about Mum: Mum as their friend, Mum being a teacher,

3

Mum being a mother, people who had told funny stories, and read out things they had written about her. Alice Bennett. My mum.

He hooked his chin over Becky's arm and looked up at her. She had pulled a hank of hair back behind one ear and was frowning slightly at the phone in her hand. Sam waggled her arm by opening his mouth and pushing his chin down onto her forearm.

'Oi, Becks, who's it from?'

She didn't answer. He tilted the little screen in her hand so that he could read it. *Lots of love, darling. Thinking of you. xxx*

Sam stared at the message. It struck him that the voice behind the words could so easily be . . .

'Becks? Becky!' She transferred her gaze and looked at him.

'It must be Vanessa,' she said. 'You know, Ness? She's in Lanzarote. She told me she would be thinking of us this afternoon.'

Sam looked at the screen again. There was no name.

'Hey, Becks, you know what I thought just then? Suppose . . . ' He shook her arm gently. 'Look at me, Becky. Suppose it wasn't your friend. Suppose it was . . . from Mum. No. No, listen, you remember that time the other week, we were in the kitchen talking about why dead people didn't have a fax or a TV channel or a website and I said why didn't they and Dad thought it was funny? You remember? Well, I just thought it could be . . . maybe it could be . . . It could be Mum, hey? Just telling us she's OK?'

'Sam!'

4

'Mum always kept saying about not being dead and being on the Other Side and in the Next World and all that.'

'Sam, stop it, that is such a weird idea.' She was looking at him now, searching his face as if she was trying to see a way through it. 'It's Vanessa. I know it is. She always calls everybody darling. Look . . . ' Becky pressed buttons. 'See? That's her number. She just forgot to put her name.' She shook his shoulder gently. 'Really, it is.'

They walked back to the crowd and were surrounded by the suits and blouses and watchful faces that Sam sensed wanted to press forward and say things. He listened to his sister saying, yes, she had to look after her two men now. But the three of them were also going to look after each other, weren't they? And yes, she agreed, Sam would be needing her more. Mr Mack appeared and squatted in front of him. Sam looked back into his serious brown eyes.

'New class soon, eh, Sam? You'll see all your friends in a few days' time. Will you go shopping for any new things before term starts?'

Sam grabbed at this good idea. 'Yes. I'm going to go into town with Geordie and Driscoll. For new football boots. And a cricket-baseball cap.'

Mr Mack nodded. His bushy ginger-and-brown eyebrows twitched. 'So, then. How am I going to cope, having you and Geordie and Driscoll in my class this year? They're your best friends, aren't they? Aye, and your mum was my best friend—well, her and Mrs Mack, that is. Lucky, wasn't I, having my best friend in the next door classroom?'

5

Auntie Pam came and pressed a perfumed cheek against Sam's face and said, 'We're off home in a minute.'

Sam found if he stood still people came and talked to him, but if he walked about as if he had somewhere to go they let him pass; so he walked quite fast, stepping in and out of people's shadows. He hurried off across to the grass again and circled a few trees, looking up into the leaves while he swung around the trunk, then he strode back in among the many little groups of talking people.

The murmurs fell away suddenly and Sam heard his dad's voice carrying across the heads of everybody. 'You'll come back to ours, then, if you want. All welcome.'

There were nods of agreement, and calls of 'Aye, Derek, ' and 'Course we will, lad.'

Sam was still for a moment. His dad had been enveloped by arms across his back, arms around his neck, heads with closed-up faces pressing into his neck and shoulders. Sam went into a long stare. Bodies shifted around him, bodies passing and repassing; suddenly there was clear open space in front of him, no people. There was sky and up in the sky a wide brick chimney with wafts of grey smoke shunting out of the top and fanning away into nothing in the blue-white air.

Then Becky was beside him; her hand was on his back. She saw his stare and turned to follow it.

'They could have waited, ' she whispered.

Uncle Roy drove them home in the Renault. Auntie Pam sat in the front passenger seat. Sam sat in the middle of the back seat. He had never seen his dad in the back of any car, ever. Now he was pressed up against the weight of his dad's big warm body, his big knee. He looked down and watched his own hands moving about being busy; they looked smart with the white cuffs showing below the end of his jacket sleeves. He glanced up once and saw his dad looking out of the window watching the residential suburbs of Sheffield sliding past: gates and front gardens and pathways and garages and porches. Other people's lives. People who had no idea what had happened to the family that was driving past.

Becky on the other side of him reached over and captured one of his busy hands and held it. A bit too tight for comfort.

Cars had filled all the parking spaces in the road and some had two wheels up on the pavement. They had to shuffle in through their own front door behind other people. Pam had forged on ahead of the queue, intent on taking over from the neighbourhood ladies who had set up all the drinks and snacks. Sam stood with Becky on the stairway for a few moments, strangers in their own house. People were politely squeezing past each other in the hall on their way between the kitchen and the sitting room; Auntie Pam's voice was strident above the hubbub in the front room; the sliding door was open and people were moving out into the garden, taking drinks and plates of snacks with them. Sam pressed back against the wall to let a heavy and perspiring man come down the stairs from the bathroom; people were hesitating in the hall, looking around, and more people were stepping in through the front door.

He felt Becky's hand cupping the back of his head. 'Sam, why don't you go up and take your suit off?'

People in the house. People from Dad's work. People from Mum's school. Becky's friends. Neighbours. Sam locked the bathroom door, ran a basin of hot water and put his hands into it and leaned forward to stare into Dad's shaving mirror. Around him the house vibrated with bodies and voices. His short mat of hair lay flat on his skull; the sticking-out ears were red because broad slats of sunlight from the window blinds lay across his face and shone on his ears. Wingnut, he got called at school. Wingnut Bennett. Through the open window he heard Auntie Pam calling to someone in the garden.

His sleeves had slipped down and the cuffs of his jacket were wet. Someone was trying the door handle.

This is a party for Mum, he told his face.

The face lifted its chin at him. Oh yes?

Yes, listen. That could be her laugh down below in all that din, couldn't it?

No. It couldn't. Mum turned into that figure in the bed in the hospital with the specially knitted cap on one side of her head to hide the part that had gone wrong.

Yes, but this is Mum's party; these people are all here for Mum.

Mum's gone to the Next World, where there's no fax or website or mobile phones, so she can't get in touch with us.

Dad had laughed at that idea. But what had Mum said?

Mum had gone into the silence.

Back in his own room he shut the door and took off his suit, put on jeans and T-shirt and then went to the window to look down onto the heads and shoulders of lots of people moving about in the garden, holding their cups and plates. She could so easily be there now, walking among them, passing around a plate of things to eat; it seemed the most natural thing to happen next—that Mum's head would appear from the sitting room door below and move out among all the people. She would laugh, and her hair would swing about; it would bounce or blow around in the breeze, so that she would peel strands of it away from her eyes.

Auntie Pam had got Becky away from everybody down the far end of the garden. Sam could see the two of them down there sitting at the round table, near to the greenhouse. And he could see the clusters of red tomatoes behind the glass. Mum's tomatoes.

He got down on the floor and pulled a large sheet of paper out from under the bed. He upended a box of felt-tip pens and they clattered and rolled everywhere. He drew big swirling lines round and round on the paper. Spirals. Whirlwinds. A staircase. It was satisfying because there were no words, and there wasn't any thinking either. He coloured-in sections, joined up lines, shaded-in blocks in different shapes.

No thinking.

Some time later the door opened and Becky and Dad were there in his room watching him.

'Sam?'

He switched pens, bent a little closer to his picture.

'You want to come on down, son. Have a drink and something to eat.'

'Not hungry.'

'Sam.' Becky was close behind his ear. 'It's the three of us now. Please. We need each other.'

'What for?'

'Pick all the ripe tomatoes in the greenhouse, for a start, ' Dad said. 'I forgot about them, last few days. They're fair dropping off the plants.'

Sam looked up. 'Why did everyone keep saying they're sorry?'

He saw a look pass between them. 'What else can they say?'

'They're apologizing, aren't they? What for?'

'What they mean is they sympathize, ' Becky said.

'I think it's stupid.' He drove the thick pen into the paper and it tore.

'Come on, Sam. Let's go down and show we're a family, hey?'

He felt gritty. Going down the stairs he turned his hard face up to Becky. 'But we're not a family any more.'

Chapter Two

Some words kept running through Sam's head: *What happens now?* Because now there was nothing much to be done. Had somebody else said the words? Or was he asking himself? After the flurry of unreal days swallowed by hospital visits, afternoons and evenings spent in hospital wards, beside the bed, first in the hospital, then the hospice, then the days leading up to the crematorium service—after all that, now suddenly there was nothing to be done.

The three of them looked at each other as they ate meals around the kitchen table, each aware of this new three-way relationship, no one saying anything about it. Becky quickly developed a tendency to hustle them to eat up, to clear plates before they had finished, to slam down a pudding while they were still chewing, and not let them sit and be quiet at all during or after the meal, not even for a few moments. Then she would retreat to the bathroom.

She spent hours in the bathroom. Sam loitered on the landing while the bath filled, breathing scents of pine and eyeing the wobbly peaks of foam, but then she would breeze past him and the door would shut and there was silence. No splashing. Sam couldn't understand what she did in there. How could anyone sit in the bath and do nothing? One time he stood inches from the door, hand raised to knock and tell her there was a phone call, and he heard muffled sounds of crying.

There had been times in the night when he had woken and heard the same noises coming from her room.

It was strange now to see Dad in the kitchen in charge of breakfast. Sam looked at the table; it seemed to have more than everything necessary on it. And Dad carrying the frying pan as if it was going to explode, transferring bacon gingerly onto plates—somehow the whole operation didn't look right in his hands.

Wordlessly, Becky made Sam wait until Dad had sat down with them before he started eating.

'I'm not going back to work until you two start school, ' he told them. 'Roy can keep things going at the office. So we'll have a few days. If there's anything you want to do.'

'Can I get the bus into town and go shopping with my friends?'

'What, stuff for school? Aye. But I was thinking of . . . outings.'

Becky, her elbows on the table, sipped a cup of tea. She glanced at her dad and took a few more sips in silence. Then she leaned across and touched his hand. 'That'd be really nice, Dad. But the three of us going out somewhere right now without Mum—that would sort of make it worse. I think we need to get used to life here first.'

Dad looked blindly back down at his plate. Sam watched them both. Becky put her cup down carefully and got up and went out of the room. When she came back it was as if she was trying to smile through a thick pane of glass.

Sam let the silence be for a few moments until he judged the bad moment had passed. Then he said, 'Can I have a mobile phone?'

'Not just yet, son. Wait till you're a bit older.'

Becky said, 'If you really really need to use one you can use mine, but not if it's just chatting to your mates.'

There were quite a lot of visitors in the days following the cremation. Dad's brother, Uncle Roy, came in the evenings and they talked business while Auntie Pam cooked meals in the kitchen and stowed them in the fridge and in the deep freeze. And Sam had his friends round to play computer games, or else they took their radio-controlled off-road trucks out onto the common lands on the eastern edge of Hallam Moors.

One evening John Mack and his wife came with a cheesecake and two bottles of wine and a big bottle of Coke for Sam. Becky and Auntie Pam cooked a shepherd's pie. Afterwards, when Dad and Uncle Roy and Mr Mack were having whiskies, Dad told again the story of how the Bennett brothers had met and married the Furnival sisters, how Roy had married Pam, and Derek had married Alice.

Sam and Becky sat quietly in a corner of the room while the adults played out their bluff jokes, spoke of everyday matters, then circled and touched the one subject everyone wanted to talk about. Sam looked at Uncle Roy, who was much thinner than Dad, slumped back across one thick arm of the settee with his arm behind Pam.

There was a silence. No one looked at anybody else.

Derek Bennett said, 'I did the contract harvesting of old man Furnival's wheat for three years before I got asked into that house. Alice were in her teens first time I went there. And Pam—'

'I was twenty-two,' said Auntie Pam, 'the first year our dad employed you. But I was already gone from the farm, so you missed out on the chance of me, Derek.' She winked. 'Too late, mate. Your brother got me first. Our neighbours thought Dad did it deliberately, getting the Bennett brothers in to do his harvesting, and then marrying each daughter off to them.'

Derek shuffled his feet awkwardly, shifting his big hands, eventually allowing them to rest on his knees.

'Aye, it were Alice I saw every year. I were only there for a couple of days, but I'd catch a sight of her around the place. She had a few goats, couple of horses. Just a young girl. She'd be home from college. But I never spoke to her. Third year I were there, the old man comes stumpin' out into the field. Shouts up to me to come in fer a bite and a sup. By God, that were a hot summer. I sluiced the dust and muck off from tap in the yard, stepped into the kitchen still drippin'. Blow me, we didn't sit at the long table, but I'm led through into this cool dining room. Great black oak beams, a cabinet full of show cups. Walnut table polished like black glass. "We'll tek it in 'ere for the cool," he says. And there's Alice with her hair up off her neck carryin' dishes. "Now then, Derek," says the old man, "how many years is it you've cut our cereals?" "Three," I says. "Six if you count Roy doing it before me." "Aye," he says. "And I think this is the hottest. Sit you, and we'll have a cool drink and some cold pie."'

14

Derek gave a small laugh. 'I sat down opposite this beautiful girl who I'd never seen close-to. The old man asked me about the business, how it were going with me and Roy. I told him we were branching out into agricultural engineering and leasing. We were just starting the transport side of the business then too. Then he shut up for a bit and let me talk to Alice. Course I knew what he was doing. Eh, but her world and mine . . . ' He shook his head. 'I listened to her tell about her teacher training college. All that student life they have.' Sam saw his dad look at the thick palm of one hand. 'I listened to her and I thought, look at me, I can't compete with college lads.'

'But you were wrong,' Auntie Pam said. 'She was a farmer's daughter first and foremost; she knew the kind of life she could have with you. Like me and Roy.'

Dad smiled. But it was a loaded smile that quickly became overloaded, so that he shaded his eyes with his hand.

There was a silence. Then John Mack spoke.

'D'you know, I reckon we take each other for granted. I mean, just the physical presence of people.' He stirred uncomfortably in his chair, frowning as he searched for words. 'What I mean is, folk sort of shine. They walk into a room and sit down and look at you. People give off a sort of radiation. Everybody does. It's who we are. And then, when they die, they're absolutely and completely gone. Silence. They're not here. So they're somewhere else.'

'Aye,' Derek Bennett said, 'but *bloody where*?'

Sam caught his dad's eye. A look passed between them.

'We had this chat once, not so long ago, eh, Sam? You started it. This was well before our Alice got sick. "Eh," he

15

says, "Dad, why en't dead people got theirselves a website?" That got us going. Well, why not? What's the matter with 'em over there? All the talent they got on their side: Newton, Galileo, Faraday, Einstein, Marconi—'

'Buddy Holly.'

Derek threw his brother a look. 'Aye, him too.'

'And Marie Curie,' said Pam.

'Yeah, all right, so anyway. Lots of 'em. All that genius. You'd think they could rig up a website. You'd think they could hack into the internet, or send us a fax . . . you'd think. You'd think they'd want to send a word or two back to us. A postcard, like. Or an email. But do they 'eck. Nothing. What are they playin' at?'

There was a musing kind of silence, and Sam got up quietly, intending to slip out of the door and go to bed. Mr Mack touched his sleeve as he passed and gave him a look, eyes-half-closed, a sort of smile, complicit. His wife rummaged in a bag and brought out a wrapped packet.

'We thought you might enjoy this.'

Sam took the packet and pulled the paper off it awkwardly because the eyes of the room were on him. It was a book with a picture of a boy sitting in the back of a cart; the cart was piled high with furniture, rolled mattresses, and junk. The boy had huge shocked eyes and was staring back the way they had come. His hands and feet were tied. It was called *Lionel's Journey*.

'What do you reckon,' John Mack said, 'writer with the shortest name in the world, or what?'

Sam looked at the cover: the author's name was Cy Trip.

Late one morning the three of them sat around the kitchen table and read again through the cards and letters. There were one hundred and forty-eight, Sam said. He continued sitting there alone after Dad had gone to the garage to work on the car; he was arranging the cards in groups: all the flower ones, the religious, the snazzy or weird ones with no religious pictures, and lastly the snaps—the identicals. At one point he looked up at Becky, who was moving around him in the kitchen preparing lunch.

'Oi, Becks, do we know anybody who's dying?'

'No. Why?'

'They could like take a message over to Mum for us.'

Becky stopped halfway between fridge and sink, lettuce in hand, and stared at him. She was looking at his hands. Sam too looked at his own hands that were shuffling and stacking and rearranging the card-pictures: the whites and pinks, the lilies and doves.

Quietly, she repeated his words, 'Take a message over for us . . . ?' Then, louder, she said, 'Yes, well, I'll ask around.'

'So will I.'

Some moments later he said, 'What will your message be?'

'To Mum? I . . . I'll have to think about it. First though, I think they'd have to be the sort of person we liked, and that Mum would like. They'd have to, you know, be on our wavelength.'

Sam twisted around and stared at her. 'We'd want to do more than wave, Becky.'

She was biting her lip. 'Yes . . . Right. So what would your message be?'

Sam looked up and stared at the wall.

'I would say, "Mum, can you see me in the dark?"'

Becky was silent for a moment, looking out of the window into the bright sunlight. 'And what would you want her to say to you, Sam?'

Sam stared, remembering.

What would I want her to say to me?

There had been that conversation, right here in this kitchen.

Dad had been washing-up after supper. And Mum was moving about putting things on shelves, wiping surfaces, jotting notes for a shopping list. And I had been sitting here; was it homework, a piece of writing? Or was I looking at a library book, something about famous people in science? Mum had stopped to look over my shoulder at what I was doing.

Who had started it? Me, probably. Reading about a scientific genius, Michael Faraday.

Dad over at the sink had laughed. Something I said. What did I say? I asked if he had a website.

'Faraday? No, he hasn't, not where he is.'

Why not? I'd thought. Or did I say it? My library book had lots of geniuses. All dead. All 'passed over to the Other Side', as Mum liked to say. Why hadn't they managed to rig up a website, or hack into the internet or fix a fax machine? Why couldn't they text us? I must have said something like that.

Dad stopped clattering plates at the sink. He looked round at me with his eyebrows raised, and he said, 'What would you want them to say, Sam?'

'They could tell us what it's like. On the Other Side.'

Mum had put her warm hand on my head. Had she said anything then?

'Aye . . . ' Dad stared through me. Thinking. 'But they don't, do they? It's silence.'

And then Mum had stood in the middle of the kitchen with a finger in the air. 'Listen,' she said.

Silence.

Dad looked at her. 'What?'

I said I couldn't hear anything.

'But it doesn't mean the air's empty, does it?' Mum said. 'Just because you can't hear anything doesn't mean the air isn't full of radio and TV and text signals. You have to tune in.'

He came back to the present and realized that Becky was looking at him, waiting for an answer.

Too many things. He would want his mum to say everything possible.

Becky put salad and fruit and bread on the table. She kept glancing outside, into the hot glare. Sam followed her glance. The grass in the back garden was shaggy and tousled. A football was just visible in it, and a busted tennis racket.

He shuffled the cards together. Becky placed knives and forks on the table and cracked out ice cubes into a jug.

'Is Vanessa-darling back from Lanzarote?'

Becky let out a sigh. 'Yes. We're going shopping before term starts.'

'I want to go shopping.'

'Go on Saturday, with your friends. I'll meet you in town.'

'Becky? Where do people go when they die? Mum always said *she* wasn't dying, only her body was dying, but she said . . . she said . . . ' He trailed off. 'She said other things, but I can't remember . . . What did she say?'

Becky sat beside him. 'Listen to me, Sam. Because you need to remember. Mum wanted you to remember. She said the only part of her that was going to be dead would be her body. Yes? And do you remember what else she said?'

'She said she'd still be herself. On the Other Side?'

'The Other Side, the Next World, whatever. Yes, do you remember her talking to us about that? How she would still be the same lovely Mum who hugged you and who kissed you goodnight? But not here. She can't be that here, and she can't do that here. But she still *is* that person—'

'On the Other Side?'

'Yes.'

'On the Other Side of where? Where is the Other Side?'

Becky got up. 'Listen, matey, today is just too brilliant for us to stay in here. Let's eat lunch and then get Dad to take us somewhere.'

During lunch Sam's eye wandered again to the kitchen message board. No one had said anything, but there was still a message, or rather part of a message, written there

20

in Mum's handwriting. None of them would pull that off and throw it away. Sam had grown so used to seeing it there he didn't really notice it any more. It was a scrawly message, like *Contact* or *Connect*, and then a number; half the paper had been torn off.

After lunch Sam's friend Driscoll turned up. Driscoll was an equally small and rather thin little boy with a gingery bristle head and glasses. He came with them in the car to Auntie Pam and Uncle Roy's house on the edge of Bradfield Moors. The boys played in the garden with the Border collie, and they lay at the edge of the pond with their sleeves rolled up and stalked newts under water with their stealthy hands.

The sudden silences in the house took Sam by surprise. Sitting at his desk, looking out of the window, or on the floor of his room absorbed among toys and books, he would come to, aware suddenly of a great quietness throughout the house. He couldn't remember silences like that when Mum was here. On one of those occasions he got up and walked through the house, looking at things in this different, aware-of-the-silence, way. Dad was in the garden, and Becky was having an afternoon out with her friends. He stood in the kitchen, aware of how still everything was. Then he went into the sitting room and looked at objects: that chair, the bookcase in the corner, a small table near the fireplace, and he thought of these spaces when Mum used to move through them. He saw her walking in the hall, always carrying something; he saw her reaching across the back of a chair to get to that shelf; and he supposed that when people died they went into the empty space between things. He ached for her to be there then, so that he could put his arms around her waist and push his head against her stomach, or lay his head on her neck and have her hand stroke the back of his head. The ache to rest on her body . . . more than an ache, a physical impulse . . . to lay his head down on her lap . . . he had never known such a yearning ever before. He sat on the carpet beside the settee and rested his head back.

Wherever Mum was, she was there now. This moment. What was she doing? She must be wanting to say something to him, and not just letting this silence lie in the air. He listened again to the empty house. And he looked again at the room of still objects; the spaces between things. The silence seemed to be waiting.

He remembered how Mum looked in the hospital bed. Her face had gone thin and grey. And her eyes had sunk back into her head; they moved to watch him, but her head did not move on the pillow. And when the tumour had started to push the side of her face out of shape she had worn a special knitted cap. It was a sort of big fluffy coloured beret that Auntie Pam had knitted and it sat on one side of Mum's head and hung down one side of her face to hide the swelling. Before Mum's speech had turned thick and blurry she had talked to Sam and Becky. They had sat either side of her, and she had held their hands and said she loved them and she would always love them and the love wasn't going to end when she wasn't there. She was going to pass over to another place, and she would still love them from there. And they were to get on and enjoy their lives and grow up good and strong and honest . . .

Sam went into Sheffield with Geordie and Driscoll on the bus. He bought a beanie hat because Geordie wore one and he pulled it down to his eyebrows. They met Becky in John Lewis and she bought them lunch with money their dad had given her. Then he went with his friends to buy new football boots.

Sunday morning. The day before school started. Becky woke early. She put on her robe and padded soundlessly downstairs and sat in a corner of the sofa in the sitting room. She had woken vaguely troubled; the silent empty room soothed her. Tomorrow was going to be a bit of an ordeal; she collected her thoughts about it. It was the beginning of her last year at school. A-level exams. The university application. And this was the end of the coping-at-home-without-Mum time, and the start of a new routine to life.

She would have talked through some of these things with Mum. Now, she swallowed it back. As with so many other thoughts and feelings. And what does this do to me? She put the unanswerable question to herself. Every time I bite back and hold in stuff that I'm desperate to talk to Mum about . . . what does that change me into?

She heard Sam coming down into the kitchen. She heard quiet sounds of cupboards opening, crockery, a drawer. He was trying not to make any noise. She got up and moved into the hall. She stood beside the banisters: from here she could see him sitting sideways-on at the table in his pyjamas. He shot a dry avalanche of cereal into a bowl, sowed it with sugar, and poured milk. He chewed. As he chewed he swung his legs backwards and forwards in turn, and he looked around the empty kitchen. She watched his little head moving about on the frail neck. What was he thinking about? Was he doing his silent talking? He was probably quite content at that moment, sitting by himself in an empty kitchen, in a house emptied of his mother.

Becky slipped away silently back up the stairs. Something had tightened in her chest and she had to force herself to take several steady breaths.

Chapter Three

'So, how was it?' Dad asked at their evening meal after the first day back at school.

Sam grumbled, 'People keep coming up and apologizing. Teachers, dinner ladies, everybody. *I'm very sorry. I'm very sorry*. Why're they sorry?'

Dad frowned. 'They don't mean to irritate, Sam. What else can they say? They worked with her; they loved her.'

'One person said something different. Here.' He fished a card out of his pocket and slid it across the table. The picture on the front was a photograph: gold evening light across wheatfields, picking out in the distance a tree and a windmill, stark white against grape-dark cloud. Inside was careful handwriting: *Sam, the ways in which you are going to miss your wonderful mother are beyond words. Coping with the death of someone you love so much is one of the biggest lessons in life, and you have to take the lesson while still so young. Miss her. Don't avoid the sorrow. It is a measure of how much you love her. John Mack.*

'I knew it would be Mr Mack,' Becky said quietly.

'Well,' Dad said. 'You want to keep that.'

Sam looked at his dad, and at Becky, and then around the kitchen. This was the first day of the altered life: the old routine, but utterly different. What happens now, he had been saying to himself. The answer seemed to be this: the old life, completely new.

Becky put down her fork and looked out of the kitchen window. 'So many people came up to me today, too. They said they were really shocked. Some of them had little brothers and sisters in Mum's class. They said goodbye to her at the end of term, then, all in like a month during the holiday, their teacher gets very ill, and . . . They couldn't believe it.'

Derek, head down, shook his head gently at his plate. 'Half of those cards we got are from children. They wrote brilliant little messages.'

'Oi, right, there's this new boy in our class. He's called Darryl but he says he gets called Dazz. He's from London. He's hard. You should see his dad. He's got a leather jacket and a baseball cap, but when he takes his cap off you can see his head tattoo.'

Becky and Derek absorbed this news in silence.

Later, clearing up after the meal, they were almost too polite with each other. Each of them reached for items to clear off the table, and they jockeyed around the sink. Derek smiled to himself. It wouldn't always be like this. Father, daughter, and son, the careful politenesses. We'll make it work, of course we will.

But we have to get through each day.

It feels like a sentence.

It hasn't sunk in yet. Sam overheard people saying that. People like Auntie Pam and Mr Mack. *It hasn't sunk in.* He knew what they meant, or he thought he did. And they were wrong. But then one day he woke up with a small shout ringing over and over in his head, *Where's my mum?* which went on all day long, and everything he looked at seemed to echo the question back at him. The hollow question.

He tried it out a few times in a whisper: 'Where's my mum?' It still didn't lead into any new thought. It just went on like a heavy egg rolling round and round in his head: *Where's my mum?*

That night, lying in bed, the egg broke.

She's dead. Your mum's dead.

'I know that. But what's dead?'

It's just very still, isn't it? Not moving—ever again.

'Ever again.'

Not moving ever again.

He made no reply to this. A pause. Then the voice tried another tack.

You're a prat, you are.

'Why?'

Because you don't get it.

'I do. I do get it. If my mum was here she'd shut you up.'

You haven't got a mum.

'Yes I have.'

Where is she, then?

He found he was sitting up and his two fists were hard balls, nails digging painfully into the flesh.

'My mum is still my mum.'

Where is she?

He shut his eyes and put his fingers in his ears. He set up a silent wail of sound, but behind it he could still hear the voice: *You don't get it. It hasn't sunk in.*

Each evening Sam took a bus home from close by the school gates. He was aware that Mr Mack, who frequently did after-school road-supervision, kept an eye on him. At the end of the second week, though, both Derek and Becky were there in the car waiting for him. He had just climbed into the back when a figure strode across from the school gates and squatted down, face level with Derek's open window.

'Mr Bennett? How you doin'? Paul Skinner.' A hand was thrust through the window.

Derek had to squirm around to get his right hand up to shake the man's hand. 'Hello? Are you a parent here?'

'Yeah. My son Darryl, we're new boys to the area. He's in your lad's class.'

There was an athletic air about the man, the way he bounced lightly, squatting on his heels. Sam saw the creased collar of an old leather jacket and the round neck of a T-shirt. A baseball cap with a long peak was tilted at a slight angle, and the man was chewing gum. It was not an unattractive face; there was a haze of faint gold stubble on the cheeks—and there was something pleasant about the eyes, a calm, almost amused expression.

'Just wanted to say, about your missus. I knew her, only brief mind, cos we'd only been in Sheffield a couple of weeks. I go to the Spiritualist Church, you know? I'd seen her there, couple of Sundays. Lovely lady. Lovely aura.'

'Oh. Yes . . .'

Sam leaned forward so that his cheek was beside his dad's headrest. Paul Skinner nodded at Becky and

28

Sam; there was an easy assurance in his eyes and around his mouth. On the jawline under his ear there was a small scar.

'She's doin' good, you know. Where she's gone, she'll be fine.'

'Ah . . . I'm sure you're right.'

'Just thought I'd say. It'll be a hard time for you, but she'll be well an' good.'

'Well, thank you for saying that.'

'Yeah. Cheers then. Take care. I'll see you.'

Later on the way home Dad said, 'So what's Darryl like, Sam?'

Sam thought. 'I told you about him. He's called Dazz and he's hard.'

'Aye, I reckon his dad can tek care of himself, too. Funny, you wouldn't have put him down as religious, to look at him.'

Becky was silent, wondering if it was true that Paul Skinner knew that Mum was fine and well and good.

There were various after-school arrangements worked out to ensure that Sam did not return to an empty house. Either Becky would be there to meet him off the bus at the end of the road with two or three others from the Primary school; or, if he wasn't met off the bus, Mrs Prythurch from two doors down would be ready and waiting in the kitchen when he came in through the door, with tea poured and a piece of home-made cake on a plate. Some days Sam would go to a friend's house for tea and be driven home later. Occasionally, though, he slipped through the arrangements. A well-meaning parent would give him a lift home straight from school; or Mrs Prythurch got the wrong day. He did not say anything when this happened because he quite liked being alone in the house, at least for that short time before Becky and his dad came home. The novelty of the silent, empty rooms interested him. He would retrieve the key from the loose brick by the drain and let himself in the back door. He would get a drink from the fridge, go upstairs and take his uniform off, then either watch television or listen to a CD or play a game on his computer. If he had an interesting piece of work to finish for homework he would sit at his desk and look out through the window onto the back garden. The clusters of red tomatoes had gone from the greenhouse now, and the lawn was still looking shaggy.

One afternoon in late September he was dropped off at home by the parent of a boy who lived two streets away. He walked quickly along the path and down the side of the house, hunched into his collar against the noticing eyes of Mrs Prythurch. The afternoon air felt thick and sticky-warm. There were hard bright clouds building in the sky, like explosive mountains. There seemed to be some immensely heavy thudding noises coming from them, or from further away below the horizon. He stood still in the silent kitchen, listening, probing the silence of the house. In the past, in his other life, he would stay on at school until his mother was ready, then come home in the car with her. This was still a novelty, being master of the empty house.

He unslung his school bag and trailed it along the hall. He mounted the stairs, the book bag bumping behind him. On the landing he stopped and looked through the open door of his parents' bedroom to his mother's bedside table. He walked in.

He hadn't ever really been in here alone before. Dad's bedside table looked cluttered; it had two paperback books, reading glasses, a mug with scummy tea dregs in it, a message notepad with scribbles and phone numbers on it, a clock-radio, a photograph of Mum's head and shoulders in a coat on a windy day, and half a packet of Polos. Mum's bedside table looked dusty and bare. In the corner of the room her dressing table was undisturbed. There were hairbrushes, perfume bottles, hand creams, necklaces and a hand-mirror all lying there. Sam looked back at the bedside table. There was nothing on it but the reading light. He seemed to remember it used to have different things on it, like on Dad's side. Where had they all gone? There was a neat stack of the small magazines that Mum used to read on the carpet beside the bed. They were Spiritualist magazines, and each one was called *The Next World*. Mum would lie in bed reading them at night. What had she said? They were about people who had passed over. People going on being people, without bodies. Ghosts then. Spirits. He went over and stood in front of the clothes cupboard; he eyed himself in the long mirror. Solemn. He bared his teeth, then tried a horrible smile. A frown. His hair was lying on the tops of his ears and overlapping his collar. He would need a haircut soon. He opened the cupboard and looked up into the cool dark folds of dresses and skirts. He swung the door and breathed faint scent. Mum and Dad's bedroom window looked out towards the moor; between the houses opposite he could see sections of bare skyline and two separate rock outcrops. There were paths there where he and his friends rode their bikes, and drove their radio-controlled trucks.

The sunlight had gone, but strange yellowish light was in the air. Thunder grumbled; the sky seemed to be adjusting itself with massive thuds and bumps. Mum used to stand and look out from here, from this actual space where he now stood. He turned back to the empty bedroom, and this time noticed the drawer in Mum's bedside table. He went over and pulled it open. A jumble of familiar small objects lay in there. Sam stirred them about with a finger: a battery clock only slightly larger than a matchbox, the stub of a packet of Tunes, Mum's wristwatch, two bracelets made of pottery beads, a pen, reading glasses on a tiny gold chain, a thin wallet with credit cards, and Mum's mobile phone. Sam pulled out the phone and weighed it in the palm of his hand. It felt satisfyingly heavy.

He had used Becky's phone several times. He knew text language. He remembered the text Becky had received from her friend Vanessa at the crematorium, and those few moments when he had imagined it coming from Mum. Mum wouldn't use text language. What would she say? *Hello, darling Sam. I love you. Don't be sad. I am fine and well and happy. Would you like to send me a message?* He pressed the On button. The screen lit up. He shifted through to Write Message. Now at last he let the strap of his book bag fall to the floor and he leaned onto the edge of the bed and held the phone in both hands. He tapped out: *mum mum mum this is sam come in mum r u receiving me love sam* He pressed Send. The empty number box appeared. What number? He stared down at the little screen. Some phones could send pictures; he imagined a hazy little picture of Mum appearing, smiling and waving—from the Other Side. He didn't really think he could do this. This game, pretending that this tiny green-lighted window could wing away a message, words to Mum. In the Next World. He clicked the phone off and looked up at the dull silvery light outside, gripped by a sudden rush of memory—Mum's voice beside his ear, her hands cupping his face, rubbing his back in the bath, tying a scarf under his chin, his face in her hair and her neck. Her smell. And the flow of her words over him. He clenched his eyes for a moment, and then made himself start breathing again.

She was always looking at him and making sure he was all right and asking if there was anything he was worried about. So she would, she *would* want to get in touch and send him a message, if she could find a way. And she would want him to send her a message. He looked down again at the little screen in his hand; the idea had gripped him; he had taken it this far and now he didn't want to just abandon it.

Mum in her hospital bed had told him they were all going to be together again, one day. In the Next World. The name of Mum's magazine. He pulled the top copy off the pile. The cover showed a misty figure in long loose clothes flying headfirst through a rainbow and heading towards meadows full of wild flowers. Inside, on the Contents page, there was a website. Contact Us. He took the magazine and the mobile phone through into his bedroom and switched on his computer. Leaden thunder-light lay over the still trees in the road, and the houses and the gardens were quiet, waiting. Rolls of thunder were coming frequently now, and there was the occasional shudder of brilliant white light. Rain wasn't far off. A sudden wind travelled the length of the road and made the trees restless. He flipped the pages of the magazine, then settled to study the Contents page. He typed the website onto the screen and clicked Search. The Welcome page began downloading in sections. There was the Contact Us box, with a telephone number.

He stared at it. That would be the telephone number of the people at the magazine. He looked down at the mobile in his hand. When you sent texts off they flew away into a corner of the screen and disappeared. Into space. If Mum was watching him, she would see him sending her a message—wouldn't she? She would read it as it flew through space? He could type out a—

The bang of thunder broke overhead followed by crackling like the splitting of a giant tree. The sky shuddered in flashes. The computer screen pinged and blanked out. Sam stared at the grey screen, then reached and switched it off at the wall.

Here were two blank screens, one in his hand, one on his desk.

He sat for a few moments, thinking, then pressed out a message onto the mobile. *mum r u there? r u anywer? I luv u can u talk 2 me? love sam xxx*. How could he send this?

It was impossible. He needed a number. For a while, moments ago, it had seemed an avenue might have opened up, a gamble—he could throw some words off into the electric spaces in-between things, shoot off a message towards the Next World from him to Mum. It had seemed possible.

Two sounds now pressed in on Sam's concentration. One was the on-rush of heavy rain filling the air outside, and the other was the sound of a car drawing up outside. A car door slammed. He could hear Becky through the growing storm uproar shouting arrangements and thanks. Sam went into his bedroom and slipped the phone under his pillow. The garden gate banged. He was at the top of the stairs with his book bag over his shoulder when Becky came through the front door holding her files over her head.

At supper Sam knew he was being unusually quiet, but he couldn't help it. He had been disturbed and stirred by the possibilities opened up by his mum's mobile; and anyway, he couldn't turn on chattiness just like that, if he didn't feel like it. Becky was moody sometimes, when she felt like it. He wanted to point out to her that the mashed potato had lumps in it, but he didn't think she would react well to that. He was considering leaving most of what was left on his plate and filling up with a sand-wich when his eye fell on the wall telephone and the message board underneath it where the jumble of scraps and cards and notes and scrawls and doodles were all collected. There was Mum's last bit of handwriting. The scrawly words . . . and the number. He twisted his head to read it. What did it say? Contact? Collect? No. Was it Connect?

Dad read to him in bed. They were on Chapter Four of *Lionel's Journey* by Cy Trip. After the storm that had devastated his home Lionel had been abducted by circus people, carried off across the plains and over the border into Mexico. He had grown fond of some of the people in the troupe, but now he had escaped and was making his way back home alone through the mountain passes where wolves stood and watched him from mountain ledges, where there were unidentifiable sounds outside the cave mouth at night, and where you did not advertise your presence to other travellers . . .

Lionel could not go on alone, though. He had to risk making contact with someone, or he would die in this land.

Dad got up and the big weight lifted from the bed. He brushed his big knuckles gently across Sam's cheek.

Sam stared up at the dark ceiling. When he was younger and his mum read to him she had played a simple game that had amused him. The light would be out but she would say, 'I can still see you.' All the way back to the doorway. Then finally just her head would be visible against the lighted strip: *I can still see you.*

Dad probably didn't even know that she did that. It was a little thing between the two of them.

He went back to thinking about Lionel. Lionel could not go on alone; he had to make contact with someone who could help him.

A sudden thought jarred him. *Making contact. Contact me on . . . ?* That number in Mum's handwriting on the notice board underneath the kitchen telephone . . . wasn't that what it said? Was that Mum's last message? *Contact number . . . ?*

When the house was silent he walked quietly downstairs to the kitchen and copied on to his wrist the list of numerals that Mum had written under the words that seemed to be *Contact number*.

Had Mum known something, even before she knew she had the tumour? Might this be Mum's last message: her contact number?

Chapter Four

Tony LeFanu drove a very large white refrigerated four-series Class D Scania rig, with a nine-litre engine, capable of hauling thirty-five tonnes fully loaded. It also had a sleeper cab and drove on an air suspension system. He was one of several drivers working a regular contract all year round to deliver perishables to outlets in the Gateshead—Carlisle—Sheffield triangle. He spent most of his days on the road and many of his nights in his cab-bunk, or else in lorry drivers' one-nighters at motorway service stations. His home base, where he lived with his wife Patty and where he managed to stay on average about three nights in a week, was a terraced house in Loxley Weir Road in the Hillsborough suburb of Sheffield, between the Loxley Arms and the Purple Haze Nightclub, and close enough to the football ground to hear the giant roars fill the sky on a Saturday afternoon.

Although born to a Maltese father and a Portuguese mother, Tony had been brought up in neither country, but in neighbouring Spain, and chiefly by his mother. He had come to England in his teens and never found it necessary to become fully fluent in the language. He got by with just the sufficient words he needed to do his job; he didn't need to do much talking anyway in his line. He was a stocky man, a little below average height, with a barrel chest, no neck, and a head of wild black corkscrew twirls. He also had a large, dark, and unruly moustache, which he never found time to trim. Tony knew he lived the typically unhealthy life of the long-distance lorry driver. But physical inactivity did not make him morose; nor did the solitary existence. He was OK with his own company. If he got lonely, he talked to himself.

This evening he was on the A69 to Carlisle with one more delivery to make, then it would be onto the M6 and back south. He was bowling along, making good time and calculating that he could probably sleep the night in the Knutsford Services lorry park when his mobile phone gave out a few rhythmic burps. (He had the ringtone set on frog.) Sometimes he ignored messages until his next stop. But if he was bored he would pull the phone out of his breast pocket and have a look, even while he was driving. Usually it was Head Office. Sometimes, but not often, it was Patty. This time he did not look at his phone. He steered the lorry through the eastern fringes of Carlisle's suburbs and delivered a hundredweight of frozen foods to the chief storage depot of a pub and hotel chain. Then he drove on, biting off squares from a Galaxy bar and smoking his favourite French cigarettes.

It wasn't until he parked his lorry on the shining wet tarmac at Knutsford Services late that night and released the compressed air in the brakes and switched the engine off that he checked his mobile. One message: *mum r u there? r u anywer? i luv u can u talk 2 me? love sam xxx*

What was that all about? Wrong number, obviously. How come this Sam used his number? He took the phone with him across to the drivers' restaurant and rest room. His mind was on a plate of lasagne and chips, with two sachets each of tomato ketchup and mustard. He sniffed his shirt as he walked. He needed a shower. His clothes reeked of cigarette smoke.

He took his food tray to a window seat and ate using a fork in one hand. He propped his tabloid newspaper against the plastic menu holder. From time to time he looked up and surveyed the area of tables, the few other solitary drivers eating.

Several thoughts occupied him as he finished his meal: Head Office, his delivery schedule, Patty. He scraped up a last spoonful of crumble and custard, drained his mug of tea, and sat back and lit a cigarette. He took out his phone again and opened up the Inbox. *mum r u there?* . . . What was he going to do about this? Erase it and forget about it. Send back: *Sorry, you got wrong number.* He looked at the words again: *r u anywer? can u talk 2 me?* What was going on here? This was a voice. A kid, surely? *r u there? r u anywer?* Who was this Sam? Boy or girl? Calling Mum. What was the story? Tony drew on his cigarette and thought. Some family break-up. It's a kid, texting the mum. There was something childlike in the words. Maybe the mum had walked out, disappeared, left the family. It happened. He had read about mothers who had just picked up their coat from behind the door and gone out, leaving a meal in the oven, the kids asleep upstairs, the husband in front of the telly, walked away from the home, everything. Where did they go? This kid wanted to know that too. Some kid, missing the mother, trying to say . . . something, anything . . . trying to make contact.

Tony knew that feeling. He stared back into a scene he had replayed over and over in his head so many times it had turned into a movie-clip, it was like an episode from a story. There weren't any mobile phones when he was a boy. There weren't any phones. Not in the mountain village in south-west Spain where he grew up. He must have been six, or seven. There had been preparations all day, because they were going on a journey; bags were packed; there had been the excitement of going off somewhere. Of course, he had thought it would be his mother and his father and himself who were going, but there had been the terrible shouting, and outside had been a car, or was it a lorry, some big vehicle, and there were comings and goings, a suitcase went up in the air and landed among melons, there had been slamming of doors, shouts and long high-pitched wailing from his mother, and then he had realized that he wouldn't be getting into the vehicle with his dad, and neither would his mother. More loose bags were thrown into a boot, or slung up onto a tailboard, and there had been more shouting, and his mother had stood with her hands covering her face but still pouring a torrent of words out, so that his father lifted his arms into the air and yelled at the sky, and then there were roaring engines; his mother was crying—crying and trying to shout at the same time. There were neighbours standing in the road. And his father had got into the vehicle and there had been thick blue smoke and choking dust and a cloud of spitting stones from the back tyres, a shower of gravel in his face. Then the dust clouds had settled and there was a silence in which the sound of the motor sank away, as though it disappeared into the ground. And he was left standing in an empty road with the white glare of the sun and his wailing mother. A mountain road, with pine trees rising in ranks up the slopes to the skylines, the stony ridges. His mother had gone into the house followed by neighbours. He had gone up the hillside by himself, up the bare rock slopes among the thin scrub plants, then higher to where the pine trees grew. And he had gone in among them. Time seemed to be slow there where they grew; and there was a special quality of silence. He had lain there on the ground in the silence, where fierce sunlight was broken up by the fuzz of twigs and pine needles, and he listened to the hiss of the high breeze up there in the very tops of the trees, and he stared down the lengths of the tree-columns into the well of blue-black sky.

He had never seen his father again.

He looked at the few words on the tiny screen in his hand. He mouthed them silently to himself. *Are you anywhere?* What was going on here?

He would have sent his father a message, if he had been a kid with a mobile. *This is Tony, your son. Come back. Pero que te pasa, cono. You please do not walk out of my life for ever. Come back.*

Would it have made any difference? He looked down at the phone in his hand. Maybe, he said to himself, just maybe, I could do some good here. He pressed Reply and began tapping. At least it couldn't do any harm. It just might brighten up some kid's day. He wrote: *Don't worry, Sam. You see you mam again. Best wishes from—*

He stopped and thought. He stared at the plastic menu holder with the name printed across the top. Then he added, *Knutsford Services*.

Chapter Five

Becky pushed open his bedroom door. She had seen his reading light.

'Hey. It's ever so late.'

Sam was lying propped against pillows, his knees drawn up. He pushed the phone down under the duvet. She came and sat on the edge of his bed.

'Were you at a party? You smell of drink.'

Becky looked up from the carpet and gave him a weary smile; and then she lingered, looking at him— through him. 'Yes. It was a bit boring, actually. What're you doing? Just sitting there staring into space? No book?'

'Becky? Have you got a boyfriend?'

'I used to have one. Luke, you remember him? But he turned out to be . . . I don't know. Maybe it was me. While Mummy was ill I couldn't really think about anybody outside our family. He couldn't put up with me being . . . ' She looked at him, then reached across and smoothed his hair across his forehead and tucked his ears so that they lay flat between his head and the pillow. 'Have you got a girlfriend?'

Sam frowned and shrugged. 'Might. Depends.'

There was a silence; Becky looked down at the carpet

again and Sam looked at his football poster on the wall: the team, and all their signatures below the photo.

He caught and held her eye. 'Oi, right, I made Dad laugh tonight.'

'That's good. He really needs us to do that. Anyway, go on. What did you say?'

'I was going through our school football team, Corey, Lane, Tad, Firoz, Keefa, Darryl, Lee, Hamid, Geordie, Craig, Chinn, Brad, and me.'

'What was funny about that?'

'He reckons they're all funny names. He said why wasn't there anybody called Pete or Dave or Brian.'

'Oh.'

'Anyway, why do we have to make Dad laugh?'

She shot him a glance. 'When I was coming up the path . . . ' She stopped and looked at him again. He saw her wondering why she was telling this, wondering if he would understand.

'Go on. I'm listening.'

'I walked up the path and I saw the sitting room curtains weren't drawn, and I just peeked in and I could see Dad in his chair. He was staring at the window with this expression on his face. And when I went in through the front door I heard him rattling the newspaper. He was shaking it out so when I came in the sitting room it looked like he'd been reading it all the time. And so then . . . ' she squeezed her eyes closed for a moment at the memory, ' . . . when I went in Dad just let down one side of the paper to look at me and ask about the party, but I knew he'd been sitting there looking out of the window—at nothing. It's night. The window's pitch black. You can't see

anything out there . . . ' Her voice rose and Sam stared at
her while she went on, half stumbling and with her nose
streaming and her voice running on and rising higher.
'And I just wanted to go up to him and put my head in his
lap and hug him and tell him it was OK, he didn't have to
try and keep up appearances with me, I love him and you
love him. But I didn't do it. I didn't do it. I let him go on
staring out into the dark.'

She put a clenched fist to her forehead. Sam watched
her shoulders shaking. He stared at her, pushing himself
slightly back into the pillows. She was bent over with her
hair falling all around her face, making muffled coughing
sounds.

'For God's sake, Mum,' she lifted a bedraggled wet face,
'look at us. You've left your two men staring into space.
Both of them. And what about me? Where the hell are
you? I'm bloody hurting too.'

When she had gone he lay and stared up into the dark. He
hadn't seen Becky like that before. And he hadn't seen his
dad staring into space, either. For a few bleak moments he
felt bereft, cut loose from the reassurance of both his dad
and his sister.

Some time later he slid the mobile out from under the
duvet, switched it off and reached down to slide it under
his bed. He had wanted to say something to Becky, or at
least hint that he had tried to send a text message to
Mum. But it definitely had not been the right time. And
anyway, what would she say to that? *Come off it, don't be so
stupid, that's ridiculous* . . . something like that. So, no,

45

maybe he wouldn't tell her at all. He would have to keep it to himself. He lay and thought about his text message. What had he said? Something like, Are you there? And now there had come back this reply from the number on the message board in the kitchen in Mum's handwriting, *Contact* . . . and that number . . . *You see you mam again. Knutsford something*. What was Knutsford? A shiver of excitement ran through his body. Imagine, though, if he could go to his dad and to Becky and hold out the mobile phone and show them and say, 'Guess what? I sent a message through to Mum. And look, I got this reply!'

He drifted towards sleep with words mingling in his head: Next World—Knuts Ford. Knuts World—Next Ford . . .

When he got in from school next day Sam heard Becky and some friends upstairs in her room; he could hear them talking over the music. He let his footsteps thump on the stairs. She turned the CD player down as he appeared in the doorway. Vanessa, cross-legged on the floor, looked up from her magazine and Jaya, lounging on the bed and flipping through the pages of an album, also looked over at him.

'Hi!—Hi, Sam.'

Sam was impassive. He said nothing. He took in the scene, then walked on to his room, dragging his book bag on the carpet behind him.

'He has good days and bad days,' Becky said quietly.

He paused on the landing, listening.

'He's coping ever so well, though, isn't he?' Vanessa said.

'He's got a sweet-shaped little head,' Jaya said. 'He should have pointy ears to go with it.'

Jaya turned the pages of the album; pointed to a photograph. 'That's how your mum looked when she taught me. Six . . . seven years ago?' Sam lingered in his doorway.

'She turned thirty-nine a week before she died.'

The music was turned up again and Sam heard the girls swapping reading materials. He went into his room and examined himself in the mirror. His ears weren't pointed at all, and he didn't want them to be. He changed out of his uniform, then tried to sit at his desk in front of the window, but the sounds of the girls' voices, their occasional bursts of laughter, and the music drove him away. He found various reasons for passing and repassing the open door to Becky's room.

Their inconsequential chatter, he found, was getting under his skin. It was something about the way they buoyed each other up, the way they could screen off thoughts by chit-chat. It was irritating. He passed the doorway and saw Jaya slide her legs off the bed and swing her heavy black hair back over her shoulder.

'Got to go. Gotta get out of this uniform. Got to get some homework done. Coming, Ness?'

Sam listened to them going down the stairs, laughing; and all the chat as they went out of the house. Something bitter slid into his mind. He went down to the kitchen. He could hear Becky outside calling goodbyes, and then the sound of Dad's car turning into the drive. He heard them come into the kitchen.

'Hey, Sam, you doing supper, then?'

No reply. Sam, head down in a cupboard, was rooting

out a single saucepan among many. He smothered their voices with metallic clanging.

Dad said, 'You two, listen. I thought mebbe we could eat out tonight. For a change. What do you think?'

Sam said nothing. He gushed water into the saucepan so that it sprayed all around the sink. He banged it down onto the stove and lit the gas. He saw Becky look at Dad. Dad was watching him. They were both watching him. Dad came over and reached for his shoulder, but Sam twisted away. He saw Dad standing in the open space of the kitchen with his jacket slung over one arm looking helpless. Sam threw salt into the saucepan. Then he tumbled an avalanche of potatoes into the sink and hosed the tap on again full blast. He yanked out a cutlery drawer and started slamming knives and forks onto the table.

'Sam,' Dad said gently, 'Sam?'

Sam was ferrying items from cupboard to table: salt and pepper, ketchup bottle, pickled onions, everything thumping, banging, slamming.

Becky went to him. 'Sam, what is it? You're going to break something in a minute. What is it? What's the matter?'

'I'm making the bloody tea, if you don't mind.'

'Sam—'

'Someone's got to make the tea. It's all right for you, if you can sit around in your bedroom with other people and play music and chat and chat and bloody chat and laugh, like everything's all right, laughing in your bedroom—So I'm making the tea, that's all.' He swung round at that moment with the teapot in his hand and smacked it into the corner of the stove. The teapot exploded and pieces crashed over the floor, fragments sliding and spinning over the tiles in all directions. Sam stood looking down at the vacant handle left in his grip.

'Whoa there, boy,' Dad said, and reached out for him. Sam ran. His feet thundered on the stairs.

He was sitting at his desk, writing, when Becky came silently into his room some fifteen minutes later and sat near him on the end of his bed and watched him, and waited. Finally he stopped and looked up straight ahead out of the window.

'Mr Mack said I could write a letter to Mum.' He spoke in a monotone. 'Mr Mack said if I felt like doing it, I could. It would be like a chat. Like talking. He said it was OK to do that.'

'I'm sure he's right. I think it's a brilliant idea. He likes you, doesn't he? He was nice to me too. We both had two brilliant teachers at that school, hey? Mr Mack . . . ' She waited.

' . . . and Mum.'

Dad drove them to a pub in Hathersage. It was an old coaching inn beside a hump-backed bridge over a small stream, with woods nearby that rose up the hillside to a moorland skyline, black against the night sky. In the bar dining area Dad got chatting immediately to a man and his family at the next cutaway semi-cubicle beside theirs. They knew each other; the man was something to do with a local livestock market. Becky too had seen a girl from her school and had gone over to the bar to talk to her. Sam eyed the family. There was a quiet mother and two children facing him, a boy with a broad-striped tuft of tinted hair down the centre of his head, and a thin-faced girl his own age in a leather jacket. He had only momentarily taken in the pair of them when he found the girl doing goggle eyes and a dropped jaw at him: *what you looking at?* He looked away quickly. He muttered, 'I'm going to the loo,' and sidled out of the bench seat.

Outside it was cold and dark, but the car park and the bridge parapet were partly lit by an orange light on a pole. The stream chuckled under the bridge; there were heavy dark shadows everywhere. Here and there sprinkled in among the ink-black trees were stars, needling pin-pricks of light. Sam took his mum's mobile phone out of his pocket. The number was written on the inside of his left wrist. The Contact number. He wasn't going to text this time, he was going to call. It was worth a try, but he felt very nervous. Under the lamp he punched in the numbers, then quickly moved into the shadow of the bridge.

Tony LeFanu was at Wortley heading home on the A629 when his mobile rang. The series of brief little electric blurts from his breast pocket only just penetrated the noise of the radio and his own whistling and the engine-roar in his cab. He pulled out the phone.

'Yep?' He turned down the music.

Sam was shocked and wordless for a moment. The gravelly voice and the whistling noise coming through the earpiece threw him. What had he been expecting? He didn't know what he had been expecting.

'Hello?' Sam gathered himself. 'Is my . . . ?'

No. That sounded wrong.

He tried another start: 'Do you know . . . ?'

A pause. Tony was on the point of saying, 'Sorry, kid, wrong number,' but he stopped himself. The small voice. The question. Then he remembered the wrong number text message. What was it? Something about a mother . . . Where was the mam, yes? And what had he replied? *Don't worries—you see you mam*. This was the same kid. Following it up. *Dios mio* . . . Options ran quickly through his mind. *Y que hago ahora?* Get rid of him, or her? Or play along? He was remembering it all now. All the questions he had rolled through his mind. What had happened? Why was the kid asking, Where are you? Some family bust-up? What did he/she want? Mysteries.

'OK. I get you message. You looking for the mam, yes?'

Silence.

'You Sam. Yes? Is you name. Right?'

Sam, standing in the cold and the shadow of the bridge under the dark trees with the phone pressed to his ear and hearing the growly voice, felt his courage draining away. How could this voice surrounded by a background wall of noise be anything to do with the Next World? Surely this couldn't be where Mum was. The Next World? How stupid could he—

'Hey, Sam. You still there?'

Further silence. Then, 'Yes.'

'You want you mam, right? I got the message. I tell you mam. I pass on message, right?'

Sam absorbed this. He ventured a further question into the darkness, into the listening space down the live phone. 'Can you give her a message?'

51

'For sure. Why not? What is you want to say?'

'Is she . . . at Knutsford Services?'

'Ah, is could be. But what I say is everything gonna be OK, you see the mam, yes?'

'Do you see her?'

Tony made a quick decision. He wanted to keep the kid on the line, not cut the connection dead and reduce this link to silence. Here was one small high-pitched voice coming out of nowhere, and there was need in it.

'Who knows? Maybe. Is lot peoples in the Knutsford Service. She is called . . . ?'

Silence.

'What her name, please?'

'Alice.'

'Sure. Alice. I see what I can do.'

'Will you tell my mum . . . Will you tell Mum . . . ' But Sam had come to the end of what he could do. Some rising tide now flooded and overwhelmed him, so that he could not speak. He opened his mouth and tried a word, but it wouldn't come because this would be like speaking words to his mum and that idea tore into him like a flame; so his word turned out to be a cough and a choke. He was possessed by a series of soundless shudders; they broke in waves through him; a kind of drenching swallowed his eyes and nose. He was aware that he had made some sort of noise that had peeled away into the night and he wondered if anyone had heard him. He broke off to grab several gulped breaths. Always in the past when he had dissolved into a wash of salty incoherence his mother had been there to gather him up. Now he was alone in the black shadow of a stony bridge beside a cold stream that ran on heedlessly into woodland darkness.

Tony LeFanu listened to the sounds of anguish.

He said, 'Hey, hey. Listen, Sam . . . *Usted vera a su Madre.* OK? No, sorry. I mean, don't worries. You see her again, for sure. Don't be sad. What you want to say to Alice?'

But no more came from the small voice in the darkness.

Tony waited for a few moments, then he switched off.

Some story.

He didn't resume whistling.

Back in the dining area Becky noted Sam's red eyes. So: he had had a little cry out there. Sam played with his scampi-bits and chips, but hardly ate anything. He did manage an ice cream with chocolate sauce. The girl opposite ignored him for most of the meal, until just before they got up to go, when she started giving Sam long looks. She got up with her family and they all edged out of their bench-seat and gathered themselves. Sam found a scrunched piece of paper dropped onto his plate. He read it under the table. *Do you want to go out with me?* There was a telephone number. He looked up. Becky was watching him with a tight-lipped, told-you-so expression.

'You heart-breaker, Sam.'

He flipped a relic of scampi off the table at her.

Chapter Six

Hi, Mum. Today is Tuesday. Christmas in four weeks. Then Sam's birthday. You won't forget it, will you? It's three months since you left us. And how about this, first a letter from Sam, and now one from me! You're being inundated with two letters. Hope you have time to read them. Is there any time, where you are? Maybe you're reading this before it even hits the page. So. What do you do all day? What are you up to? Do you still like to sit quietly and think about things? Do you still like to laugh on the phone with your friends? Do you still — Guess what I do at night? When I lie in bed I imagine your weight on the side of my bed where you used to sit. And I can feel it. Spooky, hey? Do you come when I'm asleep? Do you come and whisper to Sam? Answers on a postcard, please. Sam and Dad think you should email, or fax or something. Sam has a black joke, he says you went up in smoke. You would have said that. And me? What do I say? About your going. I say I need to speak to you so much, so incredibly much, that I have to write this letter to you. Miss Tuckwell in RE says if it was

us who had died or passed over or whatever, we would-
n't want all those people we love to stop talking to us.
So that is what I am doing. I still hear you around
the house, in the kitchen, calling down the stairs. I
could come round any corner now and bump into you
picking books and magazines up off the floor. This
letter is to you, but I can't avoid it being about me,
can I? Like — I knew you absolutely completely because
you were Mum and there wasn't one corner of you I
didn't know. And what do I know now? Absolutely
nothing. Blank. Silence. Gone. Why? If I was psychic
would you be visiting me in my head and chatting?
People said give it time and it would get easier. Time
heals. Crap. It doesn't. Time passes and more time
passes and it gets worse. People don't get over grief.
They just live on, they just don't commit suicide, they
just don't run screaming down the street, they just
don't stand on the rocks out on the moor in thunder-
storms daring God to do it, go on, do it, strike me
dead. They don't do that, they just keep surviving, and
that is the hardest thing. Going off your head is a
way out, I suppose. We get up, we get dressed, we go
to school, we work, come home, eat, sleep. We move
around each day, and we do it like we're edging
around this big hole in life. Are the edges supposed to
join up sometime? As you can see, sometimes I get a
bit angry. Most times I'm not. Mum. If I tell you I
love you, will you get the message? How will I know?

55

On Saturdays Becky did chores like washing, and her half of the ironing. Derek had offered to do the other half; neither of them enjoyed it. This particular morning Sam had gone with Driscoll to the edge of the moor to fly Driscoll's radio-controlled glider. She folded a pile of Sam's shirts and underwear and carried it up to his room. She hung his shirts for the coming week on hangers, and was on her knees folding socks and pants and vests into drawers when her dad looked in round the door.

'Becky, you haven't got Mum's mobile phone, have you?'

'No.'

'Only it's gone from her drawer. I've just been going through a few things and it's not there.'

'I haven't seen it. Did you want to get rid of it?'

'Not specially. I'd forgotten all about it, to be honest. She had one of those pay-as-you-go jobs. Isn't that what you've got?'

Becky had a thought. 'Do you think Sam might have it?'

'Aye, maybe. Would he know how to use it?'

'They all do these days, Dad. Do you want to leave it with me? I'll find out from him.'

That night Becky read *Lionel's Journey*. Usually while she read Sam played with plastic figures, soldiers or spacemen or little mythic uglies, like orcs. At other times he lay back and his eyes roamed the ceiling, or rested on her face. From time to time she would look across at him and his eyes would be focused beyond her, his mouth open. Moments later he would be asleep.

Tonight Sam was lying on his side, his cheek pressed onto the pillow, watching Lionel, exhausted and hungry,

56

moving down among the boulders and keeping watch all around for danger. By day Lionel had been following animal tracks that took him through the high mountain passes. This evening, though, he walked alone into a deserted village. Shacks had collapsed and weeds and grasses were taking over; the wind had heaped sand up against the hovels, but one mad old woman lived there alone, and she was making Lionel a meal. At night she barred her door against the wolf packs. Tomorrow he was faced with crossing a deep chasm that fell sheer to a murmuring river far far below. Strange people had appeared on the far side of the gulf who offered to throw him a rope, but Lionel did not know if he could trust them.

Becky paused. 'Sam, I've got something to ask you. If you happen to know where Mum's mobile phone is, could you let me know?' She had a sudden idea, and added, 'Only, Dad needs to pay some money, he needs to top it up, otherwise it won't work any more because the phone people will cut it off.'

Sam drew up his legs and curled into himself a little.

'We'll not send it back or anything. We want to keep it, of course we want to keep it, because it was Mum's. Have you seen it?'

Sam did one nod against the pillow. He was silent for a long while, and Becky was rising gently to go when he said, 'Oi, Becky, I've got the most best amazing secret and you and Dad won't believe it.'

She sat down again. 'Yes? What is it?'

'I can't say it right now yet. But . . . it's about Mum, about talking to Mum.'

Becky stared at him. Then she bent over him. 'That's lovely, Sam,' she whispered. 'That must make you and Mum very happy.'

He gave her a small nervous smile.

'So . . . ' Becky tried to proceed gently, 'this is to do with you, and Mum's mobile?'

Another movement of his head into the pillow.

Becky found her dad at his workbench at the back of the garage digging into a three-pin plug with a screwdriver. 'Dad, you were right, he has got Mum's mobile. He's been playing with it, using it, you know, like a toy.' She hesitated, trying to sense out how he would take this. 'I think he's been talking to Mum on it.'

Dad stopped, looked up. 'He never.'

'I suppose he must pretend to text her, or phone her, or chat to her with it.'

Silence. Dad frowned. 'Is he doing that for real or just play-acting? And is that healthy? I mean, what would one of your psychologists have to say about it?'

'They might say that he's found a way of coping, I suppose. He doesn't know what he's doing, he's still a little boy in that way—he's playing. It's the imaginary friend syndrome. He'll grow out of it. Didn't you have an imaginary friend when you were little?'

'No.'

'Well, I did. I had Angela Michaelis and she played in my tree house with me. She lived there.'

'I never knew that. Anyway, so, what's he sayin' . . . to Mum?'

'No idea. But he's obviously quite excited about it.'

'Heck he is.' Dad shook his head. 'I hope he gets over it before we all have to go on some bloody journey with him to meet Mum.'

Becky gave him a parting shot at the door. 'Don't you fancy a trip to heaven then, Dad?'

'You know what he'll say,' Dad called after her, 'he'll reckon she's at Alton Towers.'

It was a Friday evening and Sam had arranged that Geordie and Driscoll would come home with him from school; they would have tea and his dad would drive them home later. Geordie Potter came from Gateshead; he was a solemn character who lived for football and he spoke with an accent that Sam secretly enjoyed. Sam often found himself mouthing the after-echo of Geordie's words: Nuk-assle. A hoel lot a' laffs. Ah'weah an' **** yesslf. A burst of shocking white-gold hair fell over Geordie's head in a smooth arch to an eyebrow fringe.

Driscoll, who lived a couple of streets away, was a more frequent visitor to the house. He and Sam played on Hallam Moor, climbed the boulder outcrops and rode their bikes on the footpaths that meandered through the heather and the wild grasses. It had never been Driscoll's habit to speak his thoughts, or give any hint of what he was think-ing. Since Sam's mum had died he had remained, behind his glasses and behind his solemn small face, his usual earnest self. Sam rather liked that about him.

As they turned out of the school gates along with a stream of other children and walked down the hill into

Sandygate to pick up the bus Sam became aware that Darryl Skinner was walking with them. He didn't say anything to him.

At school he was called Dazz. He had no particular friends. At break and in the lunch hour he usually attached himself to a group, and because he brought a whiff of the London streets with him, in his manner and his *sarf London* accent, no one dared tell him to push off. He wore ankle-length lace-up canvas baseball boots, with black denim trousers and a jacket with imitation black leather across the back. He had two ear studs and his voice had the husky penetrative quality that comes from hard use. In the playground Dazz would walk up to any group of boys that were playing or talking and join in. He didn't play with the perpetual basketball and football crowds. Dazz didn't do team stuff. Sam occasionally saw Paul Skinner waiting at the school gates. He invariably wore dark glasses and stood, legs braced, arms folded across a charcoal singlet or T-shirt. His biceps bulged and his single heavy gold earring shone. The most interesting thing about him, though, was his tattoo. It covered his bare skull, which was sun-burned to a weathered leather-brown, and took the form of a blue ornately-decorated crucifix.

'Where we goin'?' Dazz was waiting with them at the bus stop.

Driscoll cocked a thumb towards Sam. 'His house.'

Dazz threw a cool incurious eye over Sam. 'OK.'

Sam looked away. He wasn't going to risk an ugly confrontation by telling him it was a private arrangement. Dazz carried with him the shades of the street fighter.

60

* * *

Sam was struggling with fishfingers and oven-chips in the kitchen when Becky came in. She went upstairs for a few minutes, then came back into the kitchen.

'I'll take over, Sam. You get those boys out of your bedroom and outside. Play some football. Who's the boy on your computer?'

'On my computer? He's Dazz. You remember the man who came to the car window and said his name was Paul Skinner? He's his son. I didn't invite him, he just came with the others.'

'Check his pockets before he leaves, maybe?'

Sam thought about it. 'You can't search him.'

'All right, I won't. Just keep an eye on him then, hey. I'll get you four fed before Dad gets in.'

Becky sat the four boys around the kitchen table and served up fish fingers, chips, and peas, and gave them each a mug of tea. Dazz smacked the upside-down base of the tomato ketchup bottle. Sam swept a watchful eye around the table: the chips draped in ketchup being waved around on the ends of forks.

Dazz filled his mouth and flicked his knife towards Becky, 'Iff he oar mumm?'

Sam frowned. 'What?'

Dazz chewed and swallowed. 'Is she your mum?'

There was a small uncomfortable silence. Sam wondered why Dazz's father hadn't told his son . . . but maybe there was no reason why he should.

Driscoll whispered across the table: 'She's Sam's sister. Their mum died the other day.'

Dazz chewed on, looking steadily at Sam. 'That's no big deal. There's plenty kids got no mum. My dad has girlfriends and they says to me to call 'em Mum, but I don't cos they ain't.'

Driscoll glanced at Becky and then looked with some interest at Dazz.

'Where's your mum?'

'Dunno. Walked out, didn't she. Said to my dad I've 'ad enough of you. And she said to me I've 'ad enough of you an' all, and she walked out. That's what Dad says 'appened. I was free then.'

The faces were watching him intently. Becky said, 'You were free?'

'Yeah, what Dad says. I was free years old.'

Dazz speared another clutch of chips and pushed them sideways into his mouth.

Geordie said, 'Theer's sum kids got noah dad.'

'More kids got no dad than no mum,' Dazz said.

'My dad went off for a bit once,' Driscoll put in. 'Then he come back.'

'So does mine,' Dazz said.

Sam faced him. 'What do you mean?'

Dazz gave a tired half-smile. He eyed Sam, and then his eyes flickered around the kitchen. Sam suddenly knew what he was thinking. He looked bored, because now he was having to pay for his meal by telling stuff to people who lived in houses like this and who wouldn't begin to know what he was talking about.

'When my dad does time. When he goes in the slammer. Then I goes to the fosters. Then when Dad comes out he comes and gets me.'

'The fosters . . . ?' said Becky.

'Foster 'ome.'

There was the sound of a car in the drive. 'There's my dad,' Sam said.

Dazz slid off his chair. He muttered something that was too quick and too quiet to be heard properly. It might have been 'Cheers', or perhaps, 'Gotta go'.

'What about your ice cream?' Becky said. But he was out of the back door and gone.

'We didn't check his pockets,' Sam said.

Driscoll and Geordie looked at each other. 'Ha'weah! Do ya a'weays do that?' Geordie said.

Chapter Seven

After the evening phone call from the Hathersage pub car park, Sam left his mum's mobile phone alone for a day or two. He carried it with him in his school bag, but it felt like a loaded item now. It could explode into his life. Gradually his memory of that brief upsetting exchange across the void in the night faded. The blunt voice out of the darkness had asked if he had a message for his mum. What could he say? He hadn't been ready for that. He knew what he wanted to say to his mum, but he couldn't speak it through a stranger. If his mum had come on the line, if he had actually heard his mum, that would have been . . . everything he yearned for, short of actually being with her, having her cheek pressed against his face, have her arms around him, hugging him into her warmth. But the man had seemed to know something . . . He had said he could pass on a message. So maybe he had something to do with the Other Side? Surely it couldn't be a big step then for Mum to send him a reply in her own words?

This *Contact number* . . . it had to be something special. Dad and Becky didn't seem to have picked it up. Maybe it was going to be up to him to deliver the most incredible Christmas present. News from Mum. All he had to do was keep trying—keep pushing words out there into space, keep sending messages through, so that Mum would know he was trying to reach her, so that then she would want to reach back to him. She must want to say something to him. Of course she must. He had to reach her, to tell her he was ready and waiting.

He still found it easy to imagine her voice coming down a phone line to him. And this Knutsford Services: why couldn't it be a place like the computer suite at his Primary School, where there were video link-up display screens and computers with digital cameras mounted on them . . . Knutsford Services: a place where two worlds could meet? If he could both see her and talk to her, even if it was by screen and digital camera image, from wherever she was . . . These thoughts lit golden fires in his mind. Imagine it: Mum waving to him through a screen. From the Other Side.

He put together in his head a short message. Then he wrote it down in his room on a scrap of paper. *mum, please can u fone me or txt, its urgent I want 2 spk 2 u. say were can we meet. I love u xxx sam*

If he sent that flying off into space, she surely would see what he was doing—she must read it.

Tony LeFanu was in the lorry drivers' rest room. He had his feet up and was taking a few minutes for some shut-eye. His black neckerchief was draped over his eyes and he dozed.

He had been wondering yet again just how much longer he could go on in this job. He was tired of HGV driving; he was tired of stop-start deliveries, of negotiating his enormous truck through city traffic; he was tired of service station food; he was tired of English weather and he was tired of the road. English autumn depressed him, the cold and the wet and the dying of daylight in the afternoons; he wanted the sun and the heat and the dry cloudy dust of the stony mountain roads, and the short black shadows of the midday sun on the beaten earth . . . on the tables of the village *taberna*.

Gradually over the past months a dream had grown in his head. He and Patty would give up their jobs, sell the house, and move—to the Mediterranean, to Spain, maybe the south of France. Spain was his home. He would be happy there; he could make a new life for both of them there. And it was there, he felt sure—not here, in this damp grey northern hemisphere world—there, they could start a family. Patz wasn't yet too old. It could still happen, that Tony LeFanu could be a father. He wanted very much to be a father. He was sure it could happen; he and Patty could make a beautiful child; two beautiful children. Or three!

Hold on, Tony. You don't told Patz that. Yet.

He had said nothing to Patty about this dream. He had allowed it to grow on its own. Each time he had visited it, each time he replayed it, it had developed more scenes, more pages. He had looked at the pictures—the small brilliant white house in the sunlight, the patio—a messy patio with terracotta pots and a garden seat, a workbench and tools—with the trellis and a vine growing overhead; the garden a dazzle of flowers with colours like flames, the olive trees on the hill-slope above the village, children running and shouting through the trees, running towards

66

him—a series of sunlit pages in a book: the Book of Tony and Patty's Future. He was waiting to show these scenes to her.

Waiting for what? A good-mood day. A sunny day. A day when she might smile in his face, clap him on the back, tell him he was a funny guy and she loved him and what did he fancy doing with the rest of his life?

That day was never going to come.

The phone in his breast pocket croaked.

Message from . . . He groaned. Not again. The sad kid . . . *fone me . . . urgent . . . were can we meet?* He put his head back and closed his eyes.

Why me? Why my number?

OK, I tell you why you. Is because you speak back to this kid. Sure, you try to make him (her?) feel better. How much good is that?

What, then? Is better I keep my big mouth shut? This kid is hurting because no Mam!

Tony tried to remember what he had said the other night when the kid phoned him. He couldn't remember. Maybe he should just text back: *Wrong number. OK. Thank you please. No more. You wipe off this number please.* If he did that, it would be an end to it. An end to what? To being bothered by some upset kid. Somewhere there was this family with the mam who's gone away and left them. If he sent that message then he would never know the story, how it ended. It would cut him out. He didn't want that. He had to admit this now: he wanted to be part of this child's plaintive need.

It was like all those times he passed ambulances with the blue lights and the headlamps flashing and the deafening siren that made your head ring, and the fire engines and the police cars, all of them flying down the motorway fast-lane to some story. What was the story? What happened? Who got hurt? Did they survive? What about the families? He always drove the next few miles vaguely unhappy. He could not switch off from the idea of people being hurt.

Something about the brief pleas in these text messages, something in this voice behind the words, set off echoes in his imagination. One of your parents goes out of your life and they take half your world with them.

I know all about that.

What is to do about this?

This Sam. Where is the mother? The kid thinks this is her number, so she must be somewhere.

Tony opened his eyes and looked once more at the message. The kid wanted a meeting. With the mother.

You think you can help? You what now, guardian angel? Social worker? Suddenly you the family friend, going to magic-up missing mother? Come on, Tony.

OK, he thought, OK. Say we go for it, we go for this meeting.

Why you go for this meeting?

Because I want to know the story.

OK. Honest is good, at least. What then?

But also . . .

Also . . . ?

Tony sat up and squeezed the bridge of his nose between finger and thumb. Then he clenched the black spotted neckerchief in his fist. I want to help. OK, I admit: I don't want let go the pictures in the head. The kid, boy?/girl?, sitting in some back yard, sitting in some bedroom, or on some street corner, sending out to Mam: 'I think you on this number . . . You read this words? . . . You still love me? . . . You gonna come back?' Is very sad kid. I want to help. How do I let this go?

Would there be harm in meeting the child? Sure, he/she find out that the mam is not here at the end of the phone. Then the texting stop. The truth is out. So—the kid learns about life. And I hear the story about the mam. But also, maybe I help a little.

Or maybe not. Maybe this one is real angry when they find out you just a lorry driver, you don't have access to the mam.

But they bother me with the calls! I didn't ask for that. They owe me. What is the word? Closing. Something like that. They owed me Closing on this: I am part of it.

They, now?

'Whatever. Shaddup.'

He opened his eyes, and switched on his phone. He clicked into Reply. *Am on journeys now. Soon we make contact. OK? Seeya.*

He went on looking at the message for some time. Could he maybe do something to help this kid? How dangerous was it, keeping some unknown child in hope? If Patty knew what he was doing she would have a thousand words to say on the subject.

Chapter Eight

Sam stared at the small screen in his hand. *Seeya*. That didn't sound like Mum. Was it the man who said he could pass messages on to Mum? The man who said he might have seen her. The man's voice that had answered when he had phoned from the Hathersage car park. The voice that had frightened him.

How did things work on the Other Side?

He shoved the phone in his pocket as he came into the back garden. He was immediately thankful he had done that because when he opened the kitchen door he saw Becky and her two best friends sitting around the kitchen table discussing and comparing sheets of hand-written work. Usually he would have dashed away from this threesome, but the girl with the oval face and olive skin and slow brown eyes and long shining black hair gave him such a beautiful smile that he stopped and smiled back. She was Jaya. The girl on the other side of his sister was Ness, Nessa, Vanessa, and she had a ballpoint pen stuck into a topknot of hair that spilled out over the crown of her head like a little spiky fountain.

'Hi, Sambolino,' Becky called. 'How you doing?'

'Fine. What are you doing?'

'We're doing essays. Like you'll have to do in a few years' time.'

The presence of her friends made Becky jaunty. Sam liked it when she was playful. He took a chocolate biscuit off the plate among their mess of papers. Becky got up to pour him a mug of tea. She beckoned him over to the corner by the sink, and whispered, 'Have you been, you know, talking on the mobile?'

Sam eyed her, then nodded.

'Listen, can I just have it for one moment—no, listen— it's just to check your balance, to see if there's still money in the account.'

Sam looked down at his feet.

'I promise I'll only be a few seconds, then I'll give it straight back. OK? It won't be out of your sight.'

Sam pulled the phone out of his pocket and passed it over. He watched intently. She pressed some buttons, got bleeps, saw the balance. 'That's fine. There's fifteen pounds still on it.' Then she quickly passed over into the Inbox.

'No!' He grabbed the phone. 'It's just . . . play stuff.' He picked up his bag and went out of the kitchen. He made noisy thuds on the stairs up as far as the landing, then slipped his shoes off and stepped soundlessly back down the stairs to within earshot of the three girls.

' . . . what I found out he's doing?' Becky was saying quietly. 'It looks like he's got hold of some number that he thinks is a line through to Mum.'

Silence.

Becky went on, 'I can't really get him to talk about it, but I think it's a sort of imaginary game.'

Vanessa said, 'Isn't that a bit creepy?'

71

'I don't know. Is it? You tell me. Maybe it's harmless; it's a way of coping. He's getting by on talking to her. It's what people do in church, praying, isn't it? Maybe it's just like modern praying.'

Vanessa sounded scathing. 'Should a small boy who's lost his mum go on talking to her on a mobile? No way. It's sick. Don't you see what he's doing? He's bypassing the pain. If you let him do that you're just postponing the day he has to really accept that she's gone. And anyway, what if he's making contact for real with someone, like some weirdo?'

There was another pause, then Jaya spoke.

'Come on. Surely he knows, deep down, he knows his mother is gone? He knows that in his heart. Every time he comes in through that door, there's this house empty of her. He has to accept that. And, look, he's just a small boy with imagination. He's got his own little world, and things make sense to him there. He's playing a game. OK, he's keeping her alive in his head, but is that doing harm? I don't think so. It's a fantasy. He'll grow out of it.'

Sam looked down at his grey socks on the pattern of the stair carpet. Was that all it was? Was he playing a mobile phone game with the idea of his mum being still alive somewhere?

'I just wonder if he's keeping some kind of futile hope alive?' Becky said. 'That's the only thing that bothers me.'

Back in his room, Sam sat on his bed and stared out of the window.

They had said he was playing with a toy.

I'm not playing.

This isn't an imaginary game.

I'm going to get through to my mother. She is going to see me.

At the meal table that evening Dad and Becky and Sam talked about Christmas. There had already been invitations from neighbours, and from Auntie Pam and Uncle Roy. Becky pictured their own familiar family Christmas rituals. Sam's red pillow case; the mince pies and carrot in the fireplace; the same record of carols they always played. Wherever they spent Christmas, it was going to be a hollow celebration.

'And then next thing, it'll be your birthday, Sam,' Dad said. 'What're you going to do? Do you want a party? Or do you want to go out somewhere?'

Sam considered this.

'Will you do something with your friends, Sam?' Becky asked. 'Driscoll and Geordie Potter? And what about that other boy . . . Fuzz? Do you want a party, or go out with them somewhere?'

'Dazz. Not him. And not Driscoll. He's a lameoid.'

'No! You fallen out with Driscoll? Who then?'

Sam looked at Becky. 'Your friend with the long black hair.'

'Who, Jaya? You want Jaya to come to—what?—a birthday party?'

'Yeah. She's fit.'

'Sam!'

'She flips my switch. She floats my boat.'

Dad choked on his tea and sprayed the table.

Sam knew that Becky wanted to get hold of his mobile phone. So he recharged it at friends' houses. And now for the past couple of days he had not been bringing it home at all. He kept it hidden in his locker. The December days were damp and there was a raw chill in the air, but during most lunch hours Sam would pocket the phone and make his way across the field through the straggle of boys kicking a ball, and past the knots of girls in their hooded coats and flying scarves who were keeping warm by shrieking as they ran and barged into people. Sam walked down to the chain-link fence that marked the school grounds off from some common land where he could look over scruffy long grasses, litter, and worn muddy paths. Here he switched on the phone and, though he did not try calling again, he would punch out brief messages to the number he kept printed on the inside of his wrist. Sometimes the replies were immediate; usually they came later when the phone was locked away and he would read them next day. After a few odd tries Sam's messages fell into a pattern along the lines of *were r u now? . . . is that u mum? . . . r u reading this? . . . will u b coming near us soon? . . . were/when will I see u? . . .*

Tony LeFanu found these brief enquiries out of the blue both amusing and touching. He also grew slightly flattered. Somebody's pain, somebody's need, was landing on him. He looked forward to getting yet another little question: *can you realy read my writing? Mum let me no if you can hear me.* At various times and places along his series of north-country deliveries he would pull out the croaking phone from his breast pocket, glance at the latest message, (*were r u now mum?*) and, because he was warmed-up to the idea of keeping this child comforted, or hopeful, or just cheerful, he would press out different replies, depending on where he was, (*hi sam, am stuck in long tailback . . . hey, is sunny day on moors . . . flying past angel of north . . . passing thru border country*). Tony thought that his bright and cheery progress-reports were pretty good replies to the brief pleas that appeared on his mobile. Sure, it would have to come to an end some time, but for now he reckoned on balance that he was consoling a child. He considered that he was brightening up a sad little mind somewhere, feeding the hungry imagination.

Somewhere. Where were these messages coming from? He wondered if he ever in his travels passed near to this motherless child.

Sam was half-stunned by these brief communiqués. He liked the pictures he saw in his head. He did not dare to think that this actually was his mum writing to him, yet the replies were exciting, reassuring and encouraging, and so he linked them to her. They could be her words. Who knew what things were like on the Other Side? Who was to say there wasn't travelling involved, and moving about, flying around, and getting held up? When people died they wouldn't just sit doing nothing. Mum never did that. She was always busy. It was fun imagining Mum on a journey that took her past the Angel of the North. And through Border country.

He rolled the words through his mind: *the Angel of the North. Border country*. Maybe sooner or later she was going to stop and be at a place where he could make proper contact with her. Wasn't that what this was leading up to? Surely all this phone-link exchange couldn't be pointless, with no ultimate end? He did not venture into thinking in detail about how this might happen. His mum *had* died. Sam knew that. Everything in his world told him that she had died. But she had died only to this world. Mum had said she would still be alive in her spirit, she was simply 'passing over'. Into Border country? She was still alive, but somewhere else. In the Next World, the telephone number of which she seemed to have left on the notice board below the wall telephone in the kitchen and which Sam kept printed on his wrist.

Once or twice on his way back to the playground from the perimeter fence Sam had caught sight of Mr Mack in his classroom standing at the long windows and looking; watching. Sam assumed he had been observed, being out there alone at the edge of the school grounds. That was OK. They weren't near enough to see him using his mobile phone.

One Friday afternoon Dad was there outside the school gate waiting for him in the car. There was the usual scattered posse of waiting parents at the gate. John Mack in brown duffel coat and luminous green over-jacket was watching as children climbed into cars, went off down the road in gangs, walked off with parents, or neighbours. Some of them he saw safely across the road.

76

Sam climbed into the car, but his dad didn't drive off immediately. John Mack had spotted Derek Bennett sitting nearby in his car, so when the outflow of children had dwindled to the dawdlers he walked over.

'Weekend then, Derek. Anything planned? No, me neither.' Mr Mack bent lower, so he could see Sam in the passenger seat. 'I must tell you, Sam does the job of closing down all the computers in the evenings. Very reliable, he is.'

'Aye, John. So. Kids all settled with the new teacher?'

'Sure. Children move on. They have this tremendous capacity to absorb new experiences. But it's been hard for lots of them. They'll never forget her. And I'll tell you something, Derek. Alice's going has taught kids here a very very powerful thing, bigger than you or I or anybody can imagine. It's hard to put into words. But they've had to reach deep into themselves to understand and accept, and that's more than any schooling could ever possibly do for them.'

A figure appeared on the pavement nearby. Sam bent lower to see out of the car window.

'Mr Mack? Howya doin'? Paul Skinner. You teach Darryl, yeah?'

Sam saw Mr Mack's arm being firmly tugged. Skinner was wearing a fleece zipped up to his chin. His head was a faint silver sheen of bristles. Sam was ducking and leaning to see if the skull tattoo was visible so that he could nudge his dad to see it. He thought he could make out a faint blue pattern on the top of the shaved head.

'Yeah . . . ah . . . look, I was wondering if I could just have a quick word. As you may or may not know, Darryl's been in foster care a couple of times.'

'Yes, Mr Skinner. I know that.'

'Right, well it may be that he'll be going to a foster home again in the next week or so; it depends. Thing is though, he's gonna keep coming to school here. He'll just have a different address and different folk looking after him for a while.' Paul Skinner smiled. 'Depends how the case goes. It's down in London.'

'I see,' Mr Mack said cautiously. 'You think you might be . . . away for a while?'

'Well, it's a possibility, you never know. Anyway, if it 'appens, you'll know about it, and you'll keep an eye, yeah? I know he's a bit of a lad. The others call him Dazz, eh? I used to get called Skinzy when I was at school. Dunno which is worse. It's all a bit of a laugh, though, eh?'

Paul Skinner ducked to the car window. 'Hello, Mr Bennett. I hear Dazz's been round yours for his tea. Thanks for that. See you, then, gents. Take care. Cheers, all.'

When he had gone Derek said quietly, 'Do you think we'll ever know what his London case is all about?'

'I'll let you know if I hear,' John Mack said drily.

Chapter Nine

A disturbing thought had occurred to Tony.

It had struck him that the voice at the end of all the little one-line enquiries, the voice at the other end of the single night-time telephone call, might have been a girl's.

Sam could be a girl's name these days. Sam could be a sad girl sending out these little messages: *Where are you now? . . . Can I see you? . . . When? . . . Where? . . .* She might not even be a child. Maybe a teenager. *Ave Maria Purisma!* Would she be mad when she saw him!

And that might land him with another whole set of problems. To some people he was a strange man who had sent many text message replies to a girl he'd never met . . .

He saw the scene: *I come here looking for my mum who's gone out of the family home. I fix this reunion because I think my messages are getting through to her, and what do I find—you!— a pot-bellied lorry driver with a corkscrew mop on his head and arms like hams.*

Tony looked down at his arms which at that moment were resting on the steering wheel. They were thick and quite hairy and the skin underneath the hairs was brown. The faint blue stain of his one tattoo, M A R I E, was visible, a bracelet of thin letters around his forearm. The arms trembled slightly on the vibrating wheel. *Hey!* he said to the outraged girl with the blazing eyes, *Hey, cool down, you lookin' at a married man. Absolutely! I got no bad intention, honest. I am Tony, si? Is what I am. How they say, is what you see is what you getting. Look . . .*

Here Tony paused. He was stuck. What was he going to say? He didn't know. *Come on*, he told himself, *what you going to say?* He thought about it. He couldn't think of anything. How could he defend his actions? He had encouraged her in the belief that he knew the mother, that he could pass on messages to her.

Come on! He whipped himself into an angry defence. *Hey, you know what? I was good Catholic boy. Is true. Look.* He showed her the tattoo. *See? Marie. Madre de Dios. Mother of God. I not got bad thoughts. You tell me you mam gone. You send me message, you phone me. So. I am sorry. Is true. I . . . I . . .*

Tony paused, because he saw something.

I don't want to let go this small voice. So I tell you where I am travelling. I tell you, OK stop worry, you gonna see you mam, you see her again. I try make you feel better, yes? But then I know you gotta learn that you mam ain't on this number. So I say come, you meet me here because I want to know you story, and because I think maybe I can help find the mam? Maybe, who knows?

That's it. Sorry. What I can do for you? You see you mam ain't here. So now these calls finish, hey? Sorry. Goodbye. No more calls from Sam.

Later that evening he pulled into Knutsford Services, brought his huge tonnage to a sighing halt and switched off. The battering cab subsided into a ticking silence. He dug out his mobile. *Hi, Sam, am in knutsford serv again. Maybe u come see me here. I tell u when. We try connect with Mam OK!* He would be off south again in the morning, but he would be back here before long. Time enough to fix a meeting. Buy the kid a drink, listen to the story. Maybe offer a bit of advice: where to go for help, looking for a lost parent . . . *Sure, I know what is like. One day I lose my dad; he is gone for the rest of my life . . .*

No, maybe I don't say that. Anyway, get it over. Finish. And will I be happy when this strange link with the anxious pleading voice is finally over? No, not really.

A thought crossed his mind. Maybe it was time he consulted Patty about these text messages. He would have to admit how long he had allowed it to go on. She would be mad with him. She was going to be mad with him whenever he told her. But she might have some good advice.

'Dad,' Becky said, 'those times on Sunday nights when Mum went to . . . you know, that church?'

'The Spiritualists.'

'Yes. You never went with her, did you?'

'No. It wasn't for me. I was happy for her to go. She always reckoned she were a bit fey.'

'What's fey?' Sam asked.

'Sensitive. A bit psychic.'

They were sitting round the kitchen table eating supper. Sam looked at his dad.

'Does that mean Mum knew she was . . . '

'It doesn't matter, Sam lad. She might have known. I think she did.'

He began, 'Did—?' But Becky broke in.

'Do you mind if I go?' she said quickly. 'Only, I've been thinking. I never went with her. To that church. She

81

asked me sometimes if I wanted to come with her and I always said no, and I wish now . . . Anyway, I just thought I'd like to see where she went. What it's like. See what it was she found there.'

Derek looked at her, chewed, swallowed, rested his fork. 'You go, if you want. It'll not bother me.'

'I'll bring a friend. Vanessa, probably.'

'What about me?' Sam said. 'Can I come?'

'If you want. It won't be a bundle of fun, you know.'

Derek frowned. 'You're not going cos you want to, you know, get in touch, or see if there's a message, are you?'

'No, Dad,' Becky said. 'Really. Not for that. I just wanted to sit in her space for a bit.'

'I've got a mess—' Sam began, then stopped. He saw both heads turn towards him. He looked down at his plate. How could he do that? How could he tell them he had messages on his mobile, Mum's mobile, that might be coming from the Other Side?

He started again: 'I've got a mission—to look up the Angel of the North. Do you know what it is?'

Becky said, 'Is it for a project?'

'Yes, I need a picture.'

After the meal Becky showed Sam some website pictures and Sam stared for a long time at the great figure that seemed to be a huge cross and a giant man and an aeroplane wing and a signpost all in one. It beckoned without moving: *look at me*. It also seemed to offer protection under the shadows of those great wings. Imagine flying past that.

* * *

Sam was contemplating a journey. The latest text message he had received hinted there could be a meeting; maybe soon. With this prospect came the realization that he could say little—no, not little, nothing—nothing about his texting, about the replies he had received, about possibly travelling to some place that seemed to be connected with Mum in her next existence. He had played out in his imagination the image of travelling past the outstretched arms of the Angel of the North, of passing over remote moorlands, 'Border Country'. He had pictured his mother in an undefined existence which was half the Next World and half Border Country. But reachable. Wherever it was, it was not a silent land. You *could* get messages through. The voice on the phone and the text replies had said his words could be passed on. And maybe there was this place where he could speak to his mum, hear his mum's words. Even just that. Or—at the very very least—have proof that she had received his messages. A note? A recording: her voice?

Sam knew how to use a search engine. Now he used his computer to find Knutsford Services. After a few misspellings he managed to get some responses, but nothing that explained, or that told him where it was, or what it was, or how to get there. Still, the more he focused on this place, for which there was no photograph, the more he began to form his own vague picture of it.

Knutsford Services. A place that . . . what? Looked after people? A place for people like his mum who had recently 'passed over'. Some sort of rest centre where souls on the move could stop and . . . rest? Look back? Receive messages? In the teachers' staffroom at school there were pigeon holes that held letters and notes for the teachers. Might there be a place at Knutsford where messages could be seen and read?

If there was this Other Side, then why shouldn't there be a place where the Other Side met This Side? A Border Crossing. In his bedtime story Lionel had crossed over a border. A frontier.

Knutsford Services. How could he get there? Imagine bringing the news home to Becky and to Dad. That was the most exciting and persuasive thing. Imagine their faces. Imagine how with amazement and wonder they would ask him to take them there. Imagine it being a Christmas present? Now for the first time, Sam began thinking of the preparations he would have to make if this journey really was to happen. To Knutsford Services. To Mum.

It was a big thing to do. On his own. And keeping it secret. The biggest thing he had ever done in his life. Alone at night in bed he questioned himself.

Why do you have to go to this place?

Because I started off sending messages to Mum and I got replies.

But not from Mum.

They went through the air, through space. She must have read them. So she knows. There is a connection. If I go there she will know I have come—to find her.

So?

I want her to see me. I want her to say something to me. She won't leave me with nothing. Something will happen.

This was met by an unconvinced silence.

He fell asleep under its cloud.

* * *

84

Dad had been reading *Lionel's Journey*, putting on the voices when people spoke. Doing the scary atmosphere. Becky tended to read it in a voice that did not go up and down much, but Dad obviously enjoyed dialogue and danger. He stopped at the end of Chapter 9. Lionel was drawing near to his homelands, but he was having to travel valley roads now, stony dusty tracks where you could meet all sorts of people. He had seen the dust of distant travellers coming towards him and had hidden in the grass and trees of the roadside until they passed. But hunger had driven him to approach strangers, and so far he had been lucky. He had been given food and lifts on the backs of carts, once on the back of a horse. Sam pictured Lionel walking on his own across the grassy flanks of mountains, and at night hiding on his own in the darkness, staring at the campfires of travellers.

'It's a scary story, isn't it?'

'He's a plucky lad, is Lionel. You wouldn't think it. But there's always a surprising little pocket tucked away in folk, and then something happens and bang, out it comes and you get a right surprise.'

'Did Mum surprise you?'

'Aye, she did.'

'Did her dying surprise you? Cos that wasn't Mum's decision, that was the tumour in her brain, wasn't it?'

Sam watched his dad searching for words.

'No. Not in the dying. I took on the same attitude she did. She were that calm about it. She didn't fight it, so I didn't fight it. I didn't want to upset her by gettin' angry.'

Sam nodded.

Dad looked down at the book in his hands. 'Have you been fighting it?'

'I . . . don't think so.'

'Know what? If everyone was to be told they had just a couple of weeks left, by God they'd look at every minute of every day, they'd look at every tree, and listen to every bird, and they'd tell things to their family and friends they'd never say else. They'd live that intense . . . You won't understand, but I'll tell it you anyway. This life is all about coping with two things: one is all the stuff you planned to happen not happening, and the other is all the things that you never made any plan to happen happening. That's what this life's all about.'

'What about the next life? Is that about planned things?'

'Eh, what you want me to say to that, Sam?'

'It's where Mum is.'

'Aye, well, just cross that bridge when you come to it. Get on wi' this life first. You've got plenty of it to come. Listen, do you want me to read something else?'

'No. Let's finish about Lionel soon. Then start a new book.'

'Something more like . . . real life?'

'I don't mind.' Sam was silent. He was thinking about what his dad had just said. *Cross that bridge when you come to it*. He said, 'Kids have mad adventures in stories, don't they? But they always get home in the end.'

'Usually do.'

They were quiet for a few moments.

'Becky says you've got Mum's mobile?'

Sam nodded warily.

86

'OK. Just keep an eye on the balance, will you? Tell me when it needs topping up.'

Sam was torn. He desperately wanted to tell Dad everything, all his messages, all the replies. All the amazing possibilities that burned in his mind. Of what? Contact with Mum . . . It was unbelievable. He wanted desperately to share that idea with Becky and Dad, to see their excitement, to see how they would both look at him. *Sam? You did all that, on your own?*

But it *was* unbelievable. He sensed that if he were to speak of it, if he were to let it out of his mouth, the bubble would burst. The dreams he had lived with for weeks would be wiped away. You only had to look at adults sometimes and you knew what they would say. They would look at him from their world, out of all their experience, and his hopes and imaginings would crumble into dust and be blown away. He might never send another message. Or receive one. The dream that somehow Mum was reading his words would be gone. He would be left holding nothing.

He couldn't let that happen. He couldn't let it all come to nothing.

Sam looked into his dad's face. He imagined his expression if he could tell him the fantastic news. He hesitated; the impulse to tell it gnawed at him.

Cautiously he said, 'What would you say if I said I might be able to give you some amazing news soon. And it was to do with Mum?'

'I'd believe you.'

Sam smiled and nestled down into the covers. 'Watch this space.'

Dad's big hard hand clasped his forehead for a moment. Then the light went out. Sam pressed his head back down into the pillow. Something *had* to come out of all these messages and replies. He felt it in his bones. Everything he had built and hoped for in his mind, it couldn't all just come to nothing.

I can still see you . . . Could his mum still be saying that, from wherever she was?

There were several other trucks standing in the depot parking bays, some waiting to be loaded, others about to pull out. Some were artics, some were lorries. All were white and bore the company name printed along their sides. Tony switched off, then reached for his drive-sheet clipboard and entered a few figures in the columns. He glanced across at the café. Time for a coffee and a slice of apple pie, if there was any. He glanced around the cab, gathered up some sweet wrappers and tissues, magazines and empty cigarette cartons. He looked at his tiny Christmas tree for a few moments, then switched that off. Since the first of December he had driven with a string of little coloured bulbs in his cab; they hung around the perimeter of his windscreen. The miniature Christmas tree stood up on the dash. He liked to start Christmas early.

There were two or three other drivers sitting at the tables. Tony nodded to them. He could see the top half of Patty; she was wearing a blue T-shirt and she was wiping down some hidden surface area behind the counter, squeezing out a cloth over a bowl, wiping down some more.

'Yes, love? What—?' she stopped. 'Tony!'

'Hi, Patz. You get my message?'

'Hello, love. Yes. Yes, I got that. So, what's happening? You got back early.'

'Sure. Do some paper work stuff in office, then finish. So, I wait. Then we go home.'

Patty resumed the business of cleaning out a sugar bowl and wiping salt and pepper pots. Her T-shirt said *No Credit, Cowboy*, across her chest. There was an apron grimed with marks of frying tied beneath it.

'So, how's things?'

She gave him a tired smile. 'Things don't change here, Tony, you know that. This week is last week is next week. Same guys. Same take. I still ain't earning enough so you can retire, if that's what you mean.'

Tony gave her one of his glum shrug-and-smiles. 'Listen, Patz, I don't retire in England. For sure.'

'Yeah, right, where was it gonna be, Greek islands, Hawaii? Siddown, I'll make you a coffee.'

Tony watched her lift a stack of thick white plates up onto a shelf. He sat at a nearby table; in front of him was a plastic ashtray littered with cigarette stubs and bits of rolled tomato skin, like red matchsticks. His feet crackled the white grit of spilled sugar on the floor. This was a moment—even jokily mentioning retiring like this— when he ought to put his dream in front of her, look into her eyes so she knew he was serious. At least put the idea into her mind. Think of it, Patz: let's go south to the sun, Spain, somewhere near the sea; I work; we have a family—come on, bambinos, let's be more than just you and me.

She came over and put a mug down in front of him. 'How long you gonna be over in the office? I'm closing up here at four, be ready to go soon after.'

He looked up at her. 'Patz. Serious. I don't want to go on with all these drivings for ever. I getting pretty tired of the road sometime, you know?'

Patty's cool eyes rested on him for a moment. 'Sure, well, everybody gets tired. So what? Me, I'm tired too right now.'

Tony stayed silent.

'Tony. You making me nervous. Something on your mind? Something you want to tell me.'

'No. Yes, maybe. I . . . got to go in a minute. Put invoice in office.'

Why was she looking at him like that and asking if there was anything on his mind? Had she somehow found out about his text messaging to Sam? *Something you want to tell me?* Is that what she meant? Did she know? Tony looked down at the table.

Patty went back behind the counter and began scraping burnt and blackened bits off a hotplate with a knife. Tony watched her bell of dark hair with the premature silver strands in it shaking as she worked. It felt as if something in him that had been heading always on its own in one direction had suddenly done a U-turn and looked him in the face. Sam and the textings. What would Patty think about that if she knew? What would she say?

She had stopped her vigorous scratching at the hot plate for a moment. 'So,' she called, 'what you wanna do? Give up the driving? Be a businessman? Take out shares in this café? Take me away from all this to the sun and the sea and the sand and the sangria?'

Tony smiled. 'Hey, not too far wrong. Thinking maybe we go south, out of this cold wet. Go to Spain. To south France.'

'Yeah?'

'What you think?'

Patty's well-fleshed arm shook as she scrubbed at the stove enamel. 'What do I think? What does it matter what I think?'

Tony came over to her and leaned on the counter. 'Listen, Patz. Think about it. Maybe time for change for you too. You gonna do this for ever? Maybe not. Maybe is right time now to think about different life. Maybe even think about . . . you know, family things.'

Patty stopped rubbing. She turned to him. 'Tony, love, it's a nice idea.' She spoke slowly. 'You go on having it, but it's pie-in-the-sky for me. Nice dream. OK for you, not for me. Maybe you got to have a change in your life. Me? I can't even begin to think about stuff like that. I got no choices. I got to do this.'

'Why you got no choices? What is stop you? Say you get sick. What happen? Then you got to stop. No, listen, Patz, you got good mind up here in you head, you got life. But you not got job satisfaction. Me too, so maybe we put the lives together proper?'

He liked the sound of his final words. He said them again to her where she leaned on her spread arms on the counter looking at him. Like she didn't often look at him.

'Put the lives together. Proper.'

She stared at him, a long-distance look. Then she said, 'Tony, there is one thing you're not wrong about. All day, every day, I'm dishing out baps and burgers and fries and all-day breakfasts to guys with pot-bellies out to here, arses like hippos, cholesterol and blood pressure up to heart-attack level. I'm nudging every one of them on to their terminal coronary. You understand what I'm saying? So if we're talking job satisfaction here, well, I don't get too much of that, either. And incidentally, how is the beer-and-kebab delivery business with you?'

Tony stared at her, then shut his mouth.

She touched his chest, pushed him gently. 'You and your maybe this, and maybe that. You keep your maybes. Keep your dreams. I know this life isn't up to much, but it's all I can think of at the moment, and I'm too bloody tired to think of any other kind of life right now. So I do OK. And we do OK, don't we?' She nudged him again. 'I'm just dog tired and I don't want to have to think about anything except putting my feet up and having a drink. You go on thinking about it, Tony, and leave me out of your daydreams. Cheers, love. Now you get your paper-work done and we can go home and start the weekend.'

Chapter Ten

The Pierrepoint Road Spiritualist Church was a single storey brick building in a quiet road that was lined with tall old residences, some of which had been converted to small hotels. An avenue of ancient plane trees darkened the spaces between streetlights along both pavements.

Vanessa plucked Becky's sleeve and made her pause at the entrance. Becky studied her friend, the wrinkled nose and the silent pleading look: *Do I have to do this?*

'It'll be fine. We'll just sit at the back and watch. Don't worry. Sam and me, we'll sit either side of you and hold your hand.'

Sam stared at the entrance; he watched some smart people dressed for church stepping inside. Spiritualism was all about contacting people who had died. Or them contacting you. Why did that slightly scary idea give him a shiver down his spine? It didn't seem anything like the same as sending messages off to Mum on the mobile phone, or hoping that she would send something back to him.

Inside there were the scents of flowers and books. Sam remembered the crematorium.

The three of them sat in the back row.

'So remind me again, darling, why are we here?'

Becky was silent. Why was she here? She was looking at the coloured glass window that showed a white bird flying up towards bubbling clouds and a land of sunlit mountains. Mum must have sat here and looked up at that simple picture. She wouldn't have thought it was childlike; she would have accepted that it was someone's vision of . . . what lay beyond this life.

Sam glanced at her to see if she was going to answer Vanessa's question.

Becky stared. When she spoke it was in a flat monotone. 'Mum knew from the start the tumour was inoperable. It was growing that fast. By the time she had the scan it was already too far gone for surgery. So she knew she was going to die. She wasn't afraid. Was she, Sam? She took it as fact. No fighting it. And no fear. She talked through other stuff, to Sam and me, about leaving us. But I sort of knew she was touching it lightly. You know what I mean? It was like she was making it easier for Sam and me. That's why I wanted to come here. She had something. I think she had . . . an understanding. She might have got it from this place. She might have just worked it out for herself. The thing is, she wasn't afraid of death. It was like she could see a whole big picture. I'd like to have what she had.'

Vanessa sighed and resettled her folded arms. 'When I die I hope it's quick as a flash and I don't know anything about it.'

Sam roused himself from studying the other people who had been filling up the rows of chairs. He nudged Vanessa. Things were about to start.

Suddenly he spotted a young head turning about in a fidgety fashion in the front row. It was Dazz Skinner. Sam

94

stared, fascinated for a moment. The head looked about, surveying the little congregation. Their eyes caught each other. There was a nod and a tightened mouth, which was as near a thing to a smile that Dazz ever managed. Moments later a side door opened and a silver-haired gentleman wearing heavy dark-framed glasses and a midnight-blue suit appeared, followed by Paul Skinner.

Becky stared.

Paul Skinner got up to speak. A broad and flattened gold necklace lay bright against his taut black T-shirt, and a heavy gold earring glinted; his skull bore a blue haze of light stubble with a darker patterned shadow of the tattoo beneath it.

'Evenin', folks. I've put me bling on for you, special.'

There was a rustle and some polite laughter. His talk was about living today—now, this moment. The trouble with most religions, he said, was they posted all their thinking, their faith, their hopes, in some fictitious future, which didn't exist. And at the same time they were held in the straitjacket of the past. That wasn't living. Staving off fear of death by rituals wasn't living. Living, he said, is now. Always now.

He held up a finger.

Silence.

He let it continue. Someone eased their weight and a chair creaked. Someone else coughed quietly.

Sam's eyes drifted over the other people who were sitting in front of him. Couples, some young wives, elderly ladies in twos and threes. Lots of blue hair and spectacles.

They sang a hymn. The chairman spoke about church business.

Paul Skinner then spent the next half hour identifying individuals in the congregation. He linked them with names, months, illnesses, anniversaries, and domestic details, to which people nodded and agreed. Each time he concluded and prepared to move on, Vanessa, already hunched over folded arms, shrank further into her chair.

'Please, Becks, don't let him come to me.'

There were more messages from people who had 'passed on'. There were identifying marks and habits which in life had belonged to those who were now in the Next World. There were medical conditions, pieces of advice, comfort messages, urgings not to keep sorrow alive . . .

Sam watched people in the rows discreetly dabbing eyes.

Now Paul was winding down. He paused, cast his face about in different directions, eyes half-closed, attention focused elsewhere, gathering something out of the air, perhaps, or listening.

He smiled. 'A parachute and a wheelbarrow. Sorry, folks, but I've learnt over the years not to hold back, however mad it sounds. It's usually for somebody. I'm bein' given a parachute and a wheelbarrow . . . ' He paused. 'It's for somebody here. They'll know who they are. I'm not bein' pushed to link this with anybody in particular. And there's a message: ah, this is a good one. I like this. *I'm still floatin' down the sky, and one day you'll join me*. I'm told they'll know what that means. And this one sends love. To someone . . . And just as they're going I'm gettin' this funny name: *Snitch*. So, there we are. That means something to somebody. Not my place to question it. It's for somebody else. I'm just the relay, me. That's it. Thank you.'

The chairman thanked the congregation and thanked Paul. There was a final hymn. Then a collection. The chairman led Paul off the platform.

Sam didn't see Dazz; he disappeared through the side door after his dad.

Outside, Vanessa linked arms with Becky as they ambled along the pavement under the trees. Sam, walking behind, watched them bumping each other, laughing at nothing, pretending to stumble and lurch. Girls—being silly. Just because they had spent an hour behaving and being serious.

Vanessa pulled her friend to a halt. 'So, the guy in the black T-shirt, Joe Cool, yeah? Was he the priest?'

'They don't have priests, Ness. He's a medium.'

'Whatever. He was a beefsteak, wasn't he. Are they rare? I mean, what's at stake here? Is a medium rare?'

'Shut up, Ness. Be serious. Sam? C'mon, over here. What did you think about all that?'

Sam remembered how he felt as Paul Skinner plucked, apparently out of the air, some odd domestic detail that a loved one once had, and how a blonde-haired lady sitting nearby had nodded so vigorously and smiled so hugely that her joy had turned immediately into tears.

'I believed him. I thought he really was passing messages on from the Other Side.'

Vanessa gave him a distant, sober look. 'You know what? I think so too. Know why? That stuff he said at the end, about the parachute and the wheelbarrow? That was for me.'

She paused to look at them both.

'That was my uncle Pete. No doubt about it. Dad's

97

brother. I know it was him. When I was a little girl he was always giving me piggyback rides and he used to run me up and down the garden in a wheelbarrow. I was his little toy niece.'

Sam stood beside Becky, watching her.

Becky made a gesture of impatience. 'And—?'

'He was a big-time smoker. He died when I was twelve. Got lung cancer. And that message, about floating . . . ? *I'm still floating down the sky, and one day you'll join me.'*

' . . . Yes?'

'Uncle Pete and my dad were in the parachute regiment together.'

They had resumed walking, in silence, Sam between the girls. It took Sam a minute to remember the last thing. He looked up at Vanessa.

'When you were a little girl, your uncle Pete used to call you Snitch, didn't he?'

Vanessa nodded soundlessly. Under the streetlights Sam could see her cheeks running with tears.

Sam began the Christmas holidays with rounds of visits to and from friends. Driscoll, who apparently was no longer a lameoid, came round to the house and they played on the computer, watched television, and played music. Geordie also appeared wearing a kind of zip-up tracksuit jacket with a hood which he kept pulled up, so that his shock of cotton-white hair only became visible when Becky invited him to pull the hood down. He did so, revealing that the hair was gelled and, because he had messed it up by pulling the hood down, now had to be reworked so that the spikes stood out. Sam watched this operation without comment. They planned a trip into Sheffield to do some shopping for presents.

One evening Sam came back from a day away with the news that the three of them had visited Dazz at home. Becky was working among books and papers at the sitting room table. Dad was in his usual chair by the fireplace which had a stool beside it piled high with agricultural and farming magazines. He was reading his paper.

'Oi, right, his dad's a geezer,' Sam said.

'Who is?'

'Dazz's dad.'

'What's a geezer then?' Becky asked.

'He's cool.'

Dad said, 'We saw him at the school gates talking to John Mack. I think he was hinting he might have to go back to pris—'

'Ycah, Becky and me saw him at the Spiritualist Church. Anyway, Dazz had these two other boys round, called Dwight and Dwayne. They do Gangsta Rap. Dazz says when they're big he's gonna be their manager.'

'You mean, when they're grown-up?'

'No. When they're big rap stars. They're either going to be called Black Bruvvaz, or else Mista Kurtz. Which do you like?'

Dad said, 'What's Gangsta Rap?'

Sam did a sour face and shook his head. 'Uh. Don't you even know that?' He watched his dad fold his newspaper. 'Dad? Could you get a tattoo? Dazz's dad's got this big cross thing on his head.'

Derek looked up over the top of his reading glasses. 'Sure. What design? Tractor? Lorry? Cow? Some sheep?'

Sam tried to picture his dad with a shaved head. 'Maybe not,' he said slowly. 'Dazz's dad said to us to call him Paul. He works out in a gym to keep his muscles hard.'

'Do I have to go to a gym too?'

'Oi, respec', right?'

Becky shot her dad a look. 'Sam, did Dazz say anything about his dad going away for a while?'

'Yes, his dad's going to London, and Dazz is going with him. Then he's coming back here, maybe to stay with a foster family.'

'You weren't thinking of offering . . . ?'

'No way,' Sam said.

Up in his room, Sam sat at his desk and looked at the still unsorted pile of stuff he had tipped out of his school bag at the end of term. School books, pencil case, chocolate wrappers, a half-eaten green thing in clingfilm, two dried and hardened apple cores, a penknife which he thought he had lost weeks ago . . . and a crumpled piece of A4 photocopy. Following a conversation he had had with Dazz this afternoon, this piece of paper now became precious. He felt very pleased with himself. On the last day at school he had got out an atlas of Great Britain, looked in the index and found Knutsford on the M6 motorway. Next he had opened up a national road map and looked at the countryside and the roads between the western suburbs of Sheffield where he lived and Knutsford. It fitted on to one side of A4 and he copied it. Now he had to work out how he was going to get across all that country in between.

Sam had arranged to meet Driscoll in Tudor Square, between the two theatres. The plan was to go around and choose presents for their families, then buy lunch at KFC. Sam found Driscoll standing near a small gang from school who were all perched on and around a couple of benches with skateboards under their arms. Sam stood back and eyed these characters, most of whom were a year or two older than himself, and noted their outsized denim trousers that dragged on the ground, their dull grey and green hoodies, and the beanie hats pulled down to eyebrow level. He watched them sucking on cigarettes with narrowed eyes and wondered if you always had to look like you were in a right mood if you wanted to be one of them.

Sam joined Driscoll on the fringes of the group. Both of them had reason to be wary of groups like this. Sam reckoned he got off lightly being called Wingnut Bennett. Driscoll, though, was red-haired. It had been a curse. He had plenty of individual friends, but he had learnt over the years to avoid gangs where responses were unpredictable, and where those you had thought friends could turn you over to the pack if it would score a laugh. Red hair was all some people needed to pick a fight.

Geordie and a few others of their class were gathered around another bench eating chips out of cones. Sam and Driscoll went off to buy some too and when they returned they found Dazz with a very short haircut and a zigzag pattern clippered along the sides of his head. Sam studied him.

Dazz was like a small hard rock. He wasn't in a gang, yet he was relaxed with a group. He was at home on the streets. But there was something else. Even though he didn't make overtures to other people, he had a side to him that could listen and look at you and notice you.

Sam pulled him to one side and showed him his photocopied map.

Dazz studied it. 'Bin there. Bin there. Bin there.' He poked at points on the map. Sam read the names, Chapel-Something, Buxton, Glossop.

'On your own?'

'Nah, with me dad. When he does the church services.'

Sam asked how they travelled. Bus? Train? No, they had a car.

'How do I get to . . . there?' Sam pointed. Dazz peered at the map.

'I dunno.' Dazz appeared mildly interested. 'What you want to go there for?'

Sam couldn't resist. 'To see my mum.'

Dazz looked at him and frowned. 'I fought you said your mum was dead?'

Sam decided that silence was best at this point. He watched Dazz turning over in his mind the idea of people travelling to service stations for reunions with their mums. Who may or may not be dead. Perhaps he was imagining the prospect for himself.

Dazz looked again at the map. 'Hang on a minute, we goin' down south. For Christmas at me auntie's. Me and Dad. We could give yalift, part of the way.'

Sam looked hard into the face with the shaved head. A lift with the Skinners? The journey now took a small leap into practical possibility. 'Your dad wouldn't mind?'

'Nah. I'll arx him, but he'll be cool with that.'

Sam stared at him. In his own household his dad would definitely not be cool about such an arrangement, not without fixing it up on the phone with the parent first. He could see immediately that not only must Dazz's dad not mind, he must not know either. Because grown-ups did things like phoning up and checking their children's plans with each other; parents talked and arranged times and meetings and pick-up and drop-off points. No way would Dazz's dad take Sam and drop him off on his own at or near Knutsford or the motorway and then head away down to the south of England, not without fixing up the whole thing first on the phone . . . would he?

Dazz was doing calculations. 'Today's Sat'day, right. Christmas is Wednesday. So that means Dad's goin' Monday morning.'

Sam took the plunge and made a suggestion. Was a hidden lift a possibility? Could he hide in the back? Maybe under some coats?

Dazz's eyes lit up. 'Wicked, mate. You can go in the boot.'

'Er . . . I think I'd rather hide under the coats.'

Sam now thought of two things he needed to do. Pack some things in his rucksack. And send a text message to say he was coming. Or should he call? The one time he had spoken had not been a happy experience. Over these past weeks the texts had always been friendly, encouraging. With texts, Sam felt, you were sending words off into the air, into space . . . where his mum could read them.

He could barely concentrate, trailing the shops with Driscoll in the afternoon. He bought two Christmas presents: a rainbow patterned shoulder bag with tassels for Becky, and an appointments calendar for beside the telephone for his dad. It had pictures of the Derbyshire Dales in spring. He bought himself a grey-green fleece. With a hood.

Back home in his own room he shut the door and tried on his new clothing. It had two small toggles dangling on laces. He pulled up the hood. His face in the mirror peered back at him out of the small oval.

I could be anybody.

He hunched his shoulders a little and stared back at himself, unsmiling.

One day to wait.

Becky and Dad were going to be cross, there was no avoiding that. But then. When they heard the news of where he had been, and why he had gone in secret, then it would be worth it. He had to leave them a note. They would read it and look at each other in surprise and then wonder what the secret journey was all about, and they would wonder what was the amazing news he had to tell them when he got back. They would be worried about him, but he could text them.

The final version of his note that he pinned on Sunday

night under his Bennett Bros Agricultural Contractors &
Hauliers lorry paperweight read:

Dear Dad and Becky, do not worry about
me. I am fine. I have gone on a secret jurney.
I will not be away for long. Gess what! I will
be back before you know with amasing news.
(For Christmas). I am hopping to bring back
some speshal news that will make you very
very happy and delited. Love from Sam. XXX

He read it over, then added a PS. Sorry but I keep
the mobile swiched off so I dont get bothred.

When Becky came up the stairs later that night, his
light was off and he was pretending to be asleep. It was at
that moment, while he sensed her bending over to look at
him, that he remembered the note. It was lying out in the
open on the desk. But the room was in semi-darkness; she
wouldn't see it. He lay still, but he could not stop his
eyelids from fluttering minutely. She paused for a moment,
then left him. Sometimes he liked to feign sleep.

Hi, Mum. So: it's Happy Christmas. This is another
of your daughter's one-way-only progress reports.
Like one of those family newsletters people put in
their Christmas cards. So, what's to say? It's
Christmas and you've gone away. So it isn't going
to be Christmas at all. Only it has to be, for Sam
and for Dad. OK, and for me as well.

Sometimes it feels like you're so far off. And
sometimes it seems like you're warming the back of
my head. And sometimes it's like, Stop fooling

105

yourself, people _are_ totally wiped away when they die. It's — oblivion. So stop playing the same game your little brother plays.

Progress Report for you: Becky is working hard at school. The outlook for A level in English and History is very good; but in RE Miss Tuckwell thinks she is not reading widely enough. Becky's social life remains on hold. Actually, it's no-holds. Nobody holds me, and I hold nobody. Nobody has asked Becky out for ages, because she is still fragile goods. Rebecca Bennett, yeah, used to be quite a laugh, but she's a bit of a difficult number now: I mean, what could you talk to her about?

Mum, listen to me, please: I'm worried about Sam. He's got some private game going on with you and your phone. He tries to say things to me and to Dad about it, but he's holding something back. Please have a look inside that funny little head for us. I don't really understand what's happening in his imagination. I see him round the house, and he's in some world of his own, I can see him saying things silently to himself. You know all about it? Of course you do. So what's going to happen? He'll grow out of it? He won't grow up a frustrated mummy's boy, sort of pathetic and lame? No. Good. Of course he won't, he's our Sam. Thanks.

We keep the house going. Cooking. Washing. Dusting. Boring.

There is something else about the house. This sort of quietness, which is the absence of you. Dad tries to lighten things, I see him being bright and cheerful for Sam and me, but he can't keep that up and it lapses and this silence slides back. Like it's waiting there in the background, and any noises we make — they're just a momentary ruffle on this pool of universal silence. It's not gloom, and we're not depressed. It's like once the sun shone bright and warm, not _on_ a place but _in_ a place, in our house, and now the sun's gone. Bereaved. We are the bereaved.

I have times when I feel happy.

All I have to do is get through the rest of my life. Oh my God.

Chapter Eleven

The morning of twenty-third of December. Sam tugged his curtains half open and let in a little grey light. It was dry and cold outside; the trees and gardens were held in a windless stillness. He paused on the landing, in his baseball cap and new hoodie top. Becky's door was closed. Behind him, the note lay on his desk. He got down the stairs and out of the house to the buzz of his dad's electric razor in the bathroom.

The sky was a dull white blanket of cloud. It was very cold. Sam looked down at himself: trainers, jeans, grey top. I look like anybody, he thought, like most other kids. He hefted his rucksack on to one shoulder and set off through the suburban streets. Dazz had not really known what time he and his dad were leaving; he had thought maybe it would be after breakfast, after they had loaded up the car.

This was the day before Christmas Eve. He didn't know how far this day would take him, but he posted a faith into that same thin air that had received all his hopes and texted words over the past weeks—a faith that he would complete his mission, whatever that turned out to be, and be back in his home by Christmas.

He was still his mother's son. *She knows what I'm doing.*

In morning living rooms of the houses he passed he caught the glisten of silver tinsel, of coloured bulbs glinting among tree-needles. People were waking up to the excitement of their own houses changed into decorated caves. And presents to come. He found he was clenching a fist: *there had to be something waiting for him at the end of this journey*.

He approached the Skinner house slowly along the opposite pavement. There was a rumbling and he looked behind him just in time to see a train passing over the railway arch at the end of the street. He slowed and loitered for a while behind some parked cars; he didn't want to be spotted by Paul Skinner and have the plan dumped right at the start. There was a gap in the line of cars opposite where the Skinners' old Ford Sierra Estate had stood when Sam was here before. He studied the blank face of the little terraced house, its grey lace curtains. Those curtains were very still; there was no movement and no light showing behind them. He waited on the kerb, watched the small movements of traffic and people passing at the end of the road. What to do?

Some minutes went by. Sam looked at the empty car space. A suspicion grew in his mind. He walked some distance down the road, then back again. The house was still and silent. No sign of life. He crossed the road and knocked on the door. Silence. He knocked again. They had gone without him. And then with a sudden little rush of insight he saw what a childish idea it had been all along. He and Dazz between them, they had talked it up and believed each other. But it was never going to happen, was it? Hiding away in the back of the car . . . ?

How realistic was that? It had been a boys' idea, just another of those plans that didn't have lasting power. Real life had nosed it out of the way.

Sam shouldered his pack. At the end of the street he paused and pulled out of his pocket the folded photocopy map. Sheffield western suburbs were here . . . Knutsford Services, there.

He looked at all the country in-between. A testing moment. He could chuck this whole scheme and just make his way back home. What would that do to him? He reached into himself: did he have the resolution to go on . . . on his own?

Paul Skinner had felt vaguely uneasy from the start of the trip. At first he said nothing and put it down to just having woken up feeling out of sorts. But then he started voicing his disquiet, because it seemed the further on he drove the more uncomfortable he felt.

He glanced at his son in the passenger seat.

Dazz felt his dad's scrutiny. 'What?'

'I dunno. I'm not happy. I'm gettin' this funny feeling, and it feels like it's connected with you.'

'I dunno what you're talking about.'

'I'm not happy. I don't know what it is. But the further we go the more I feel I didn't ought to be driving in this direction. You got any ideas about that?'

They stopped in a café in Eyam for coffee and a dough-nut. Paul said nothing. Experience had taught him to let his intuition work at its own pace. Dazz looked at his dad. Paul was looking down, stirring his coffee. He had a new haircut and Dazz could study the swirly design of the crucifix tattoo on his dad's skull.

He said, 'It's a pain having a dad who's psychic. Other kids get away with stuff.'

Paul smiled. 'Hey, you don't know how much I let you get away with.'

'Yeah, right.'

Paul waited, then reached across and gripped his son's wrist just as he was putting a doughnut to his mouth.

'What? What?'

'Come on, Darryl. Why am I not able to drive on any further? Cos we can't, not till we settle whatever it is I'm pickin' up.'

Dazz sighed. His dad never called him Darryl. He put the doughnut back on his plate. 'It's to do with that little kid, Sam Bennett. Yeah? Kid with the sticky-out ears? You've seen him, he's bin round our house with his mates.'

'I know him.'

'Yeah, well, I was fixin' to give him a lift. This morning. With us. He wanted to get to some place, I forget where. He said he was going to see his mum.' Dazz shrugged. 'I dunno what he was up to. That's just what he said. Only, we went early before he arrived.'

'*You* were giving him a lift? How come I didn't know about this?'

'You'd have . . . made problems, wouldn't you? He was just going to curl up in the boot, or hide under some stuff in the back. That was the idea.' He paused. 'Look, it wasn't anything to do with me. It was his idea. Well—all right, it was both our ideas. He just arx'd me. I said we could lift him part of the way, and you wouldn't need to know. Can I eat my doughnut now?'

Paul held his son's gaze. 'Did his dad and his sister know about this? No, I thought not.' He was silent, thinking. Then he said, 'So, we've gone without him. He's not in the boot now, is he?'

Dazz shook his head. 'Honest.'

'So when we was leaving, what did you think? Cos that little kid was going to be turning up at our house and we not there.'

Dazz shrugged. 'I just reckoned he'd see we was gone and . . . go back home.'

'Where was he heading for? Did he tell you?'

'He pointed to some place on a map. I can't remember where.'

Paul stared off in the distance for some while.

'We have to go back.'

'*What?*'

'Think about it, son. Look at what we know, and his dad and his sister don't know. They probably think he's off playing round one of his friends' houses. And they won't know till he doesn't come home tonight. The boy has gone off by hisself. We have to go back and tell his dad.'

'Why do *we* have to do it?'

'Cos at this very moment you and me is the only ones who know.' Paul leaned forward. 'He told you he was going to see his mum? That right?'

'Yeah'

'Son, his mum died four months ago.'

112

Dazz stared at his dad. 'I know. That's what they said when I went round his house for tea. But it's what he told me. I said to him, what you wanna go there for, and he says, to see my mum.' Dazz looked down at the table. 'Sometimes I say my mum's dead, too. Sometimes. It saves explainin'.'

When Becky got in that evening she found Derek trying to open a frozen pizza packet in the kitchen.

'Give it up, Dad, I'll take over. What is it with men and sealed plastic wrappers?'

He stood back watching her nimble fingers. She slit the cellophane, flipped the waste bin lid, switched on the oven, rattled out plates and cutlery onto the table, shot frozen peas into a saucepan and pushed a drying cloth into his hands. She still had her coat on.

'If you're going to stand about looking spare, just dry those things and lay the table, will you. I'm going upstairs for a minute. Filthy city. Look at my hands.'

Some days I am on top of things. Some days I am, Derek Bennett said to himself. He filled the kettle and stood staring out of the window at the dark garden.

Becky breezed back in. 'No Sam yet, then?'

'No.' Derek glanced at Becky. 'Round at Driscoll's, is he?'

Becky froze over the kitchen table, salt, pepper, and a ketchup bottle held out in mid-air like an offering. 'I don't know. I thought you knew where he was. Didn't you take him round there this morning?'

'No. He was still asleep when I went to the office. At least, his door was shut.'

She stared at her dad. 'When I got up I looked in and his room was empty. I thought he'd gone in the car with you, that you'd dropped him off at one of his friends.'

Derek sighed. 'Dammit, he's never done this before. Listen, can't we phone him on that mobile?'

'Dad, you don't know how many times I've tried phoning him. He's that canny he keeps it switched off. It's the one thing he's very cagey about. Don't ask me why. He's only just able to admit that he's even got it. My friends were saying it's not really good for him, letting him go on with whatever little game he's playing.' Becky looked at her dad. 'You know what I'm talking about? Playing with the idea of talking to Mum? I mean, what if he's dialling some real number and there's folk somewhere getting these messages . . . '

'Aye, well, that's something else. Let's just sort this out first.' He picked up the kitchen wall phone, then scanned the list of numbers pinned to the noticeboard. Becky squeezed past him and went back upstairs. He was in mid-dial when he heard her thundering back down again. He stopped when he saw her face.

She thrust Sam's note at him, crumpling it against his chest.

Chapter Twelve

Sam got onto a bus heading along the Eccleshall Road. He got off at the City Hall and sat for a while on a seat by the fountains. Cars and buses growled past. People with somewhere to get to were walking past. From time to time a scatter of pigeons flew up into the cold grey sky. Sam tried to think out a pathway. He had to make a decision. Now. Because all the weeks of picturing things in his head, all the hopes, had built up and could not be ignored. Not now. Not after all he had ventured so far. He got up and slung his pack on one shoulder and walked. He crossed the Inner City Ring Roads and the roundabouts and eventually he found his way down the slope to the railway station.

His finger had traced the thin black line that swooped like a whip across his map between Sheffield and the nearest city to Knutsford: Manchester. He bought a pie and an apple, and he asked the ticket seller behind the glass screen to point out the platform.

Platform 2, the Hope Valley Line. There was a delay. The next train would be in two hours.

There was a heavy grey sky over the city and the air was bitingly cold.

Sam looked up at the huge blocks and cubes of the city skyline, and he thought of his dad gone off to his office at

115

Bennett Brothers Agricultural Contractors and Hauliers. And Becky, on the phone to her friends. A pang of homesickness spread like a stain over his thoughts. When would they realize he had gone? It's not for long, he told them silently. You'll know why I went, and then you won't be cross and upset with me any more.

When he left the warmth of the entrance hall and went out onto the platform he found about ten other people all standing apart from each other, waiting. He watched the small train trundling steadily over the tight strands of silver rails towards their platform. He felt helpless; he was in the grip of events that seemed to have their own momentum now. He had to go through with this.

It was a little two-carriage train with an aisle down the centre. There were two teenage girls sitting near him, and a man with a plastic travel cage which he kept on the seat beside him. Sam could see a silent tabby cat inside sitting up and looking anxiously out through the grille. He sat beside a window and as the train set off he looked intently at the brief views of the city blocks and high roofs that opened for a moment and then were shut off as they passed brick walls and high buildings.

This was a moment. He had never ever done anything like this before. He thought of Dazz going off early that morning and probably not giving him a second thought. That didn't matter. What about Becky and Dad? When would they read his note? Puzzled and intrigued, they would look at each other and wonder what on earth could this fantastic thing be that their Sam was hoping to bring home? Never would they guess what was in his mind. Sam felt a shiver twitch his shoulder blades; his hair

116

tingled up behind his neck. What *was* in his mind? Expectation: something to come at the end of all the messages addressed to . . . wherever his mother had gone. It had to be done. There was no avoiding this journey. It was Fate. What was it people said about some things being in your stars? Sam looked across a cityscape of roofs and aerials. Then it all blacked out as the train entered a tunnel.

When the dull day reappeared the city had gone; there were sheep fields and high skylines. The little train squealed to a halt at Grindleford and then Hathersage, and there were meadows with dry stone walls around them, and hill slopes densely wooded with thickets of twiggy broomsticks.

Sam became aware of a tall figure standing at his side. He looked up into the conductor's face.

'This all there is of you?'

Sam looked up at him blankly. He held up his ticket and the conductor looked at it.

'Is it just you?'

'Yes.'

'How's that, then?'

Sam swallowed.

'I'm going . . . to my mum.'

The conductor was a young man; he wore an orange day-glo body-jacket and he had straight sandy hair which flopped over one eye. He looked at Sam with expressionless eyes for several seconds. It was impossible to tell what he might be thinking. Finally he said, 'Is that what the arrangement is, then? Your mum's having you for Christmas?'

'I . . . haven't seen her for a long time.'

'Did he put you on the train, your dad?'

Sam suddenly felt intolerably hot. His T-shirt was sticking to his back. He wasn't controlling his face very well. Was the conductor noticing? He blinked and his eyes roamed the carriage. The two girls were watching him in silence, their big eyes were outlined in black, and they had long lashes.

'No.'

The conductor studied Sam's ticket again. 'What happens at Manchester Piccadilly? Will your mum be meeting you?'

Sam was unable to look away from the cool staring eyes; he was also unable to reply. Silence. The conductor silently handed the ticket back and moved on up the carriage. Sam looked up and met the eyes of the tabby cat on the seat across the aisle; it was standing up in the container on all four legs, bracing itself against the sway of the train and looking at him. Sam could see its mouth opening regularly, but there was no sound above the rackety noise of the train.

The train was passing through meadows that rose to steep heights of rusty bracken, a conifer wood and then bare mountain skylines. There were tiny figures of walkers up there, pacing along the edge against the sky in red and blue jackets with packs on their backs. They were prepared for anything that could happen. They would have whistles and tents and emergency chocolate. Sam looked down at his bag beside him. He didn't have a whistle or emergency chocolate.

He studied the map. There would have to be another train from Manchester. It would go to Wilmslow, and

Mobberley. Then Knutsford. He wondered if the conductor was going to ask more questions. If he would make things difficult at Manchester.

He felt a sudden rush of excitement. He wasn't going to be stopped; he was going to do this. Mum knew he was coming. His words *had* been getting through to her, of course they had. She knew what he was doing, she knew he had set off; she knew he was travelling towards her. Now.

He reached for his mobile phone.

am on my way. i will b there 2nite. mum, can u b there? mum? let me know. love sam

He sent it.

The two girls in the corner were peering into plastic shopping bags with Jangles printed in big letters across the outside. One of them looked up at him, saw him watching, and did some fast, bright-eyed blinking at him.

Tony stood on the hydraulic tail-lift of his lorry, pressed the green button and rose in the air. The interior walls of the lorry were diamonded aluminium and they glittered, reflecting the interior light. It was very cold. He wore heavy-duty leather gloves to carry the packs of frozen burgers, chicken drumsticks, and pizzas over to the platform. He descended with the last batch, two hundred kilos of frozen doner kebab, hand-trolleyed the smoking cardboard boxes through the vast doors of Northern Wholesale Foods Distribution Warehouse, got the delivery note signed by a depressed supervisor with a heavy cold, wished him a Merry Christmas and walked back to his cab.

He had been on the road for four days, doing the long round of pre-Christmas deliveries. He had been in Nottingham and Stoke today. Tomorrow he had Bradford and Leeds. Then it was home—to make some sort of Christmas for himself and Patty. Right now all he wanted to do was hit the road and get some miles under his wheels before he turned in for the night.

It was late, though. He switched on and started up, and while the engine growled around in its comfortable rhythm, and the air in the cab warmed, Tony looked at his tachometer and did some calculations. He ought to stop before Manchester.

Then he switched on his phone. He had kept it off for most of the afternoon to give himself a break. Two messages and one missed call—from Patty. The first message was . . . He groaned. *I am coming 2 knustford serv. I will b there tommo. can u b there. love sam.* Coming to Knutsford? Now? No. Not now. Not at Christmas. This was sent yesterday. He looked at the second message. *am on my way. i will b there 2nite. mum, can u b there? mum? let me know. love sam*

No No No No . . .

He looked at the time this was sent. Today. A few hours ago. The kid had left home; was on his way there now.

Tony stared down through the spokes of his steering wheel.

This had been coming. He saw it now. All the time, through all the days and weeks of this little game of consoling the unknown kid, this had been coming. He just never imagined it coming now, at Christmas.

He looked at his two options. One was to ignore this message and just drive on and do the last few deliveries

120

tomorrow and get home and chill out and get on with Christmas. And the other was to send a reply. Saying what? *No, Sam, forget it. Go home. Another time.* Tony rested his arms on the steering wheel and stared out into the winter dusk. It was near to freezing. The forecast was for snow on the high ground in parts of the north. He stared over his little lighted Christmas tree that stood in the middle of the dashboard, into the bleak emptiness of a black tarmac lorry park. Between the orange sodium lights on their tall poles and the low clouds, a flock of starlings was steering itself about the sky, tilting and veering as it travelled in a broad sweep round and around. Tony watched it as it changed its shape, bulbing and then elongating—a shoal of flickering black birds wheeling around the winter sky. What did they know? All they had to do was keep together; do the movements along with everyone else. Human beings knew too much.

There was of course a third option. Go there. To Knutsford Services. See this Sam. Tell him/her: *You got the wrong number*. He knew he must hold up his hands. *Yes, sorry. You blame me. Is OK. I let you send all this messages. Why I do that? I think maybe I can help. You looking for you mam? Why, please? What happen? Maybe I help . . . ?*

This was what he thought would happen, eventually. But not now. Now was not the right time. Was it?

No. Running these options through his mind, he knew which he would do. The easiest—ignore it. Erase. Drive on. Forget it. He pushed the gear-shift, released the brakes, revved the engine and rolled. He was dog-tired. He didn't need to take on somebody else's problem right now.

Chapter Thirteen

Manchester Piccadilly was all glass and roof-struts, big-spacey echoes and polished stone floors as smooth as ice. Walking along the platform, Sam was overtaken by the conductor from his train, the black satchel containing the ticket machine slung over his shoulder. He disappeared among the thin tides of drifting people that strolled across the concourse. Announcements billowed overhead under the girdered roof. He walked around the smart shops and looked at a stall selling individually wrapped bagels and muffins and cookies and pastries. He sat for a while on a bench and watched people passing. He watched a girl trying to run to a platform in stilettos, her long hair undulating behind her.

It was lonely, travelling by yourself. It was only bearable, he decided, if there was something waiting for you at the other end.

After a while he roused himself. Overhead a bank of television screens listed all the Departures. Knutsford: Platform 10. Another little two-carriage train. Sam sat beside a heater that blew stale hot air onto his legs.

As soon as the train pulled out clear of the station Sam saw that the daylight had almost gone. Stockport was a darkened plain of gold and white lights under low reddened and orange clouds. Acres of cars were ranked in front of supermarkets, and people were trundling trolleys laden with their Christmas food shopping across the dark tarmac. The train ran along the backs of houses and Sam stared into the tiny lighted scenes of other people's lives. The woman at the kitchen sink, the boy in the white T-shirt in his bedroom, the pockets of glitter in sitting rooms where a decorated tree stood by a window.

None of this lightened Sam's spirits. Every little house seemed to be just holding on to a tiny bit of Christmas with a decoration; every little house was an illuminated pocket of hope. The early winter night cloaking the city seemed to compress the people in their lighted rooms. He looked at himself reflected in the black glass of the carriage window. Ears, small bare head, cropped hair lying thick and flat across his skull, watchful eyes. You are Sam Bennett. Where are you going? Are you happy? Where could people go to be happy and free? He bared his teeth. It wasn't a smile.

The trip to Knutsford took forty minutes. He got off and found himself on a small platform that ended in the black arch of an overhead road bridge. The few people who got off with him quickly dispersed, and Sam watched the lights on the rear of the little train disappear into the tunnel. Now what? Slowly he climbed a flight of steps up to a road, a T-junction. There was a sign pointing to Town Centre and Motorway.

A boy behind the counter at the petrol station directed him. Knutsford Services: a twenty minute walk from the roundabout.

Traffic was incessant and Sam walked into a relentless

confrontation of travelling headlights. At his shoulder tonnages swept past, the winds of their slipstreams brushing his face. He walked past darkened front gardens and lighted windows along an avenue of houses. There was a large open grassed area to his right. Street lamps were strung out along the roads. Every minute or so the night sky thundered overhead and the lights of an aeroplane that moments before had taken off from Manchester airport burned under the clouds, then they tilted away and disappeared into the darkness. Sam's eyes watered in the cold; the end of his nose and his ears were stinging.

Then the houses stopped, and so did the street lighting. He found he was walking in the dark along a narrow pavement beside a hedge that from time to time clawed at him with invisible brambles. Beyond were open fields on either side. Now he relied on intermittent headlights to show up the way through the shadows along the path. In the distance across the fields the roar of the motorway was growing louder. He could see a line of orange lights on high poles.

It wasn't so far, and it hadn't taken long. Sam stood beside the hedge and looked ahead. This road he was standing on crossed over the motorway. He could see a perpetual stream of lorries and roofs of cars sweeping by under the lights. But facing him, among the trees on the opposite side of this road, there was a gateway and a small back-road that led to the Services. He could see the petrol station and the car park and the lorry park, and beyond them a building with a section that spanned the carriageways of the motorway in both directions and joined another building on the far side.

He stared at the small village of lights. Knutsford Services.

He crossed the road and walked down towards the lighted car park area. He checked his mobile. A voice message from Dad: *Please, Sam, ring home . . .*

I will. Soon.

No reply to his last message. Yet.

Derek Bennett telephoned the police at 8p.m., moments after Becky had thrust Sam's note into his hand. By the time a police patrol car drew up, forty-five minutes later, at the kerb, Derek had left two voice messages on Sam's mobile and Becky had left one, plus a text. Both told him they were very very worried, both pleaded with him to phone home and tell them where he was.

The presence of two uniformed policemen sitting at their kitchen table upset Becky more than the nagging anxiety of Sam's absence. Up till now, behind her worry was the constant reassurance that at any moment there would be a phone call, he would walk through the door, a parent would call and everything would be explained. But the bulky black flak jackets of the two men, and the smell of the cold night air they brought in with them, and the intermittent crackles of static, brief, unintelligible messages from their police radios unnerved her.

She watched them as they read again through Sam's note.

. . . I have gone on a secret jurney. I will not be away for long . . . I will be back before you know with amasing news. (For Christmas) . . . some speshal news that will make you very very happy and delited . . .

'Sam's not a runaway,' Becky said. 'There hasn't been a row, or anything like that. Honestly, we're . . . we're not exactly happy, but we're getting on with life, since our mum died.'

'I see. And that was . . . ?'

'Four months ago.'

The older man nodded, looked down at his notes. 'Would that be affecting the lad still? I mean, Christmas an' all, he might be visiting a grave, or some place where she used to be, perhaps?'

Derek Bennett sat at the kitchen table opposite the two policemen. 'There en't any grave. My wife's ashes were put around the flowers in the crematorium gardens. That's what she wanted.'

Becky hesitated. 'There is one thing.' She glanced at her dad. She could see his brow furrowing, trying to guess what she would say. 'The phone-game, Dad? You know, with Mum's mobile . . . ?'

She told them about the mobile phone and the excited hints he had given her at night when he was in bed. The two policemen watched her. The younger of the two, who had fair hair, seemed only a year or two older than herself. Derek confirmed that Sam had hinted at some mysterious surprise-to-come to him, too.

'Did he actually send off messages?'

'I . . . don't know. I couldn't see to check. He wouldn't talk about it, and he never let me see his phone.'

'So he could in theory have been sending messages and getting replies, and you wouldn't necessarily have known about it?'

'Replies from . . . ?'

'Replies from whatever number he was punching into the phone.'

Becky looked helplessly at her dad.

'Look,' Derek said, 'our Sam is a sensible lad, he's not one to play with danger. He's in a secure home here. All he's been doing, we think, is using his mum's cell-phone to . . . well, to pretend to talk to her. At least, that's what we think's been happening. It seemed harmless, eh, din't it, Becks? He's an imaginative little lad. He's happy in his own world. Sure, I reckon he has fantasies. But that phone is just a toy. He's been pretend-talking to his mother, that's all. We reckoned it were harmless.'

There was a silence in the kitchen. Becky could read nothing in the policemen's faces.

'He's got a computer, has he? You don't think he might have been using a chat room?'

'No,' Becky said. 'I know my little brother; he hasn't been doing that.'

They went off with the addresses of Driscoll and Geordie and Dazz Skinner in their notebooks, promising to return within two hours. When they had gone Becky said to her dad, 'The only person Sam would ever arrange to meet . . . '

' . . . would be his mum,' Dad finished for her.

They stared at each other.

She went up to Sam's room again. She had been here several times already this evening without putting the light on. It was calming, standing in his room at the window in the half-light reflected from the streetlamps and looking out onto the shadowed gardens, trying to put out feelers to sense where he was. He had sat here at his desk in front of this window thinking out some little plan. What was it? Where? Where had he gone?

. . . *I have gone on a secret jurney. I will not be away for long* . . .

What was it that he thought would make them all happy and delighted?

Downstairs, Derek couldn't bring himself to sit down anywhere. He prowled from kitchen into the hall, into the sitting room. He went outside into the garden and walked up and down to the greenhouse and back over the freezing grass. He didn't notice the cold. Sam, our Sam, gone off by hisself to make contact wi' Alice. Surely that must be it. Good grief. He ground his knuckles into a palm, and once he hammered his forehead gently with a balled fist. I never noticed; I never saw it coming. This has been building for how long? And we missed it, *I* missed it. He tried to tell me once, I remember. And now . . . where *is* he? Where does our Sam go to find his mum?

The two policemen were back in an hour, saying that a description of Sam had been circulated to police in a hundred mile radius. They agreed to a mug of tea. This time they pointed out the name-flashes on their flak jackets: George and Shilling. It was their surnames. The elder was Constable Allan George, and the younger Constable David Shilling.

They sat themselves back down at the kitchen table.

Constable George looked up. 'Mr Bennett. There's two and two we've not put together yet. Firstly, the lad's telling us he's taken himself off somewhere, and wherever it is, it's a place where in his own words he says he's going to bring you news . . . he says you'll be amazed and delighted.' He paused. Becky looked at her dad, who was leaning in the corner against the sink with his arms folded and his back to the kitchen cupboard. 'What kind of news could that be?'

Derek Bennett stared at him.

'And secondly, Sam has been play-talking to his mum on her mobile phone.' Constable George paused. 'Do you see what I'm saying? He thinks he's been talking to her, or sending her texts. Now whether you call that just imaginative play, or whether you think it's something more serious, I don't know. And now he's left home to go and bring you back "amazing" news . . . ' The policeman looked up at the ceiling light over his head. 'He's gone looking for his mum, hasn't he?'

Derek stared at a spot on the table surface. He sighed. 'Aye. 'appen he's taken his play-actin' game, talking to his mum, and gone too far wi' it. He's . . . what? . . . he's away off to mek contact with his mother.'

'So where does a little boy with imagination go if he thinks there's a chance of contacting his mum again?'

'I've bin hammerin' my brain. I've no idea. He's not a dotty kid, constable. Our Sam is a normal sane boy.'

Nobody stirred. Becky listened to the flick of the second hand on the kitchen wall clock.

'Did you know that the Skinners, father and son, aren't at home? Neighbours say they took off early this morning.'

'You think . . . Sam might be with them?'

Becky watched her dad. His face was drained.

'Sit down, Dad. I'll make some more tea.'

Both policemen were silent. Constable Shilling, the one who looked to be in his early twenties, also had fair eyebrows and was trying to grow a fair moustache.

'What company is his—your wife's—phone registered with?'

Becky told him.

'If it comes down to it, we can run a check on his calls and texts. You'll have to give us the number. You've tried phoning him, of course?'

Becky gave him a tired smile. 'Like he says in the note, he keeps it switched off.'

'Have you sent him a text message?'

'We've both left him messages, voice and text, asking him just to phone and let us know he's all right.'

The policemen stood and were gathering papers and tucking ballpoint pens into breast pockets when the door-bell rang.

Becky froze.

Derek dived down the hall and scrabbled at the door catch. Becky stared at nothing, listening to the voices at the door. She looked up and found the eyes of the younger policeman on her face. Her dad was back a moment later followed by a solemn-looking Dazz, his eyes shaded by the long brim of his basecall cap, and his dad. Both wore jeans, trainers, and zipped-up fleeces.

'Well,' said Constable George, 'if it isn't Paul Skinner.'

Skinner nodded, gave a tight smile. 'Constable.'

Derek looked intently from one to the other. 'You've got news of Sam.'

Paul Skinner looked at the two uniforms, then at Becky, then back at Derek Bennett. 'Up to a point.'

Chapter Fourteen

On the left, a river of moving red lights in surrounding blackness, every one of them sailing away in a slow curve and disappearing from sight. On the right, white headlights spangled in the glass and approaching slowly—until they drew near to the overhead walkway where Sam stood, when it seemed that they suddenly picked up speed and swept by under his feet.

He was standing at the midway point along the corridor in front of the huge plate glass window with his bag on the glossy plastic rail and his mobile phone in his hand. The lights were mesmerizing. He didn't know how long he had been standing there, staring, not knowing even if he had been thinking of anything.

The Services had surprised him. When he entered there were bright lights shining in an area of red plastic tables and chairs where nobody, not one soul, was sitting; and there were bright lights in the shop where walls of magazines and books and stands of sweets stood waiting for a crowd of shoppers, but hardly anybody was there, only one or two browsers. No one played on the games machines. A tall glittering Christmas tree stood in a corner of the concourse, its branches festooned with coloured lights and tinsel and little parcels. He had gone up the stairs and found the walkway across the huge road, and another seating area with a Marks and Spencer's Food Shop, and a Harry Ramsden's Fish and Chip stall, and a Ritazza Coffee Counter. Silver and green Christmas decorations hung from the ceiling, and at the far end in the children's corner another Christmas tree winked coloured lights. He walked the short corridor above the road to the opposite flight of stairs and at the bottom found a mirrored arrangement of exactly the same shops as those on the other side. Beyond the entrance doors was another car park, with only a few vehicles standing on the black tarmac.

The motorway roared like a torrent.

Knutsford Services. So what had he pictured? He didn't know any more. These clean and bright spaces, these eating areas for travellers, the empty rows of tables and chairs ready for families. What was to be made of this? Inside, the lights were too bright and the roar from the road was too incessant to allow him to think anything about why he had come here.

He had gone into the toilets and stood for a moment among the mirrors and the washbasins, near a section of floor that was partitioned off and being mopped by a thin impassive man whose expression and slow movements depressed him even further in this odd, alien place.

He ran a basin of hot water, rested his fists in it and looked up. He felt sorry for the face that stared back; its cheekbones stuck out, and so did its ears. The eyes looked solemn. Empty. He bent his head before the eyes started asking him questions and splashed water onto his face. This made him do some hard panting into the basin, as if he wanted to rid his lungs of stale air.

After that he had climbed back up the stairs to the overhead walkway. He had stopped then, and faced the dark window and the black night that was filled with an incessant low thunder. And the twin rivers of lights: red lights and white lights crawling slowly across the heavy plate-glass window.

He was supposed to be hungry; it was well past supper time; he was aware of feeling hollow, but somehow he didn't feel like eating anything. There was too much to absorb. Too much to deal with. Three or four of the tables in the upstairs area were occupied. Two business men in dark blue suits; a middle-aged couple; two lovers who were stroking each other's faces. One woman busied herself behind the coffee counter. A young girl with dark hair and a thin face was behind the Harry Ramsden shelf; she wore a narrow white cap on one side of her head, but it didn't fit well. She was manoeuvring a huge piece of battered fish onto a plate; it had a tail that curled up in the air.

Time passed and after a while he ceased to think about his position on the walkway above the centre of the road. He stared out into the contra-flowing sets of headlamps and tail-lights, seeing them, and then not seeing them. They were like the Christmas lights he had been looking at in people's living rooms. Moving lights in the dark night. They meant people, sitting in their seats, travelling, heading *to* somewhere. People down there, but not really anywhere, travelling. It was going to be Christmas Eve very soon. The flow of vehicles was endless, the stream of cars and white vans and lorries with taut rubber-skin sides rippling in the wind, red brake lights winking on and off.

He stared into the black glass.

What is there here for me? I've come this far. What else do I have to do? What else is there? He took a deep breath, shuddered, faced the question that his ghost-self in the glass asked: *What did you think you could find here?*

My mum knows I'm here.

So?

(Silence.) I'm not going away.

A wave of weariness swept over him. He looked at his watch. Past bedtime. Past *Lionel's Journey* time. He smiled to himself. Sam's Journey.

He watched the moving lights. *I'm here*, he thought. *Mum? I'm here. You must know I'm here. It's over to you.*

There had to be some purpose to this. Everything he had done, sticking to that decision to leave home and travel to this place by himself, and keeping it all secret. Why had he done that? Because he had sent words into space for his mum to read. And by coming to this place, where replies had come from, he was forcing something to happen.

Something *had* to happen.

The ghost face stared solemnly back at him from the black night. He stared out beyond it into the huge darkness.

Mum? I'm here. Can you see me?

Chapter Fifteen

The forecast had predicted freezing overnight temperatures, and tomorrow the likelihood of heavy snow on high ground in the midlands and the north. Tony switched his radio off and dug into his breast pocket for the phone and pressed Call on Patty's number.

'Yep? Hi, Tony.'

'Patz. So? Happy Christmas.'

'Not yet it isn't. You know what time it is? Where are you?'

'Ah, South Manchester. You?'

'Where d'you think? It's Christmas Eve tomorrow. I'm at home, making sausage rolls.'

'Hey, you work tomorrow?' There was a silence. 'Patz?'

'Sorry. I'm trying to watch telly and talk to you and roll pastry. Yeah, I do the morning, then finish. The last drivers should be back in the depot by then. You too, Buster.'

'Sure.'

A humming drone came out of the phone at Patty's ear.

'You're not supposed to drive and phone, you know that?'

'Sure. Listen, Patz. This gotta be the last time I do winter lorry drivings. I want the sun. I need sun. I hate these black wet road, these cold cities, these cold nights.

Please, Patz. Let's make the mind to go. We make new lives for us, away from here.'

'Not that again? Gimme a break, Tony. I don't want to think that pie-in-the-sky stuff.'

'We go south, together. To real south. Spain. You think?'

'Yeah, yeah. Keep dreamin', Tony. You got anything else?'

Patty listened to the whistle of Tony's cab, and to his throaty breathing. She said, 'I'll see you in the morning, yeah?'

No reply.

'Bye, Tony.'

Flecks of sleet were smacking onto the windscreen and sliding away in the slipstream. How could she not at least say she would think about it? How could she not want to move away from this muddy cold dark country? He clicked on down through his Inbox. This last text message from the Sam person: *am on my way. i will b there 2nite. mum, can u b there? mum? Let me know. love sam.* He looked at his watch. It was late—just past eleven o'clock. The signs for Knutsford Services were beginning to appear.

Stuff Knutsford.

He did not ease his foot from the accelerator. And he did not shift over from the middle lane. He felt angry and trapped. If Patty wouldn't try to understand how he felt, then he was cornered.

Tony thundered on. The engine was humming and he was shifting the miles. He had tried to put a note of bright hope in talking about his dream to Patty. He just didn't know how to cope with her weary inability to respond. So, what am I? Disappointed? More than disappointed.

Bloody angry. He wanted to hit back. He drove on in the whistling cab above the engine, with the string of coloured Christmas lights around the huge double windscreen, and the miniature lighted tree on the dash, and the noise of rushing wind outside, and the multiple thundering of the great wheels.

A car flashed him in his mirrors: *move over*.

Stuff you, too.

He still had his phone in his hand, his thumb on the Erase button.

He droned straight on—in the centre lane at sixty-eight mph past the slip-road to Knutsford Services.

Stuff Knutsford. Esta acabao! Get over it, Sam—whoever you are.

He wiped the last Sam text.

As he did it, the phone gargled briefly. Text: *Mum. r u reading me? I am here now now now now. xxx sam*. Tony swore softly. Aloud, he said, 'Forget it, kid. It's over.' The lighted buildings of Knutsford Services were sliding past on both sides of the motorway. He put his thumb again on the Erase button and thundered under the building that spanned the road, with its brilliantly lit windows, the glimpse of a decorated corridor. As he passed under it he looked up and surveyed the narrow lighted passage that spanned the whole carriageway above him. It was empty.

No, not quite empty.

Empty, except for one small figure standing midway, directly over the central barrier, so that north- and south-bound traffic swept both ways beneath.

'Cono!'

He took his thumb off the Erase button.

He thought fast. Press call? Speak to the kid? No. Don't frighten him/her. This one you got to play careful.

He pressed out: *Tell me where u r EXACTLY*.

One minute later came the reply: *in midle of tunel over road*.

'*Dios mio*.' Tony began quietly to swear.

Then he began a debate.

'Is impossible. Can't do it.' (*You got responsibility, Mister lorry driver*.)

'I didn't start this.' (*But you make it go on*.)

'Is too late. This bloody place behind me now.' (*So how long you think that small kid stay there, waiting? For Chrissake! Is not too late*.)

Tony clenched his fist and thumped the wheel.

'*Aaaaaaaaaa*,' he yelled to no one.'*Madre de Dios!*'

There followed a couple of short sentences which were made up of most of the bad English words he knew. He stared bleakly at the road. The unrolling belt of reflectors that never came to an end sucked back under his lorry. He was motoring. He was putting the miles away. But he shouldn't be here, he should be taking a rest. At Knutsford. Fate had decreed that he should have stopped at Knutsford and he had gone against Fate. He drove on, refusing to permit the accusing thoughts.

Shut up. Don't think. Drive.

But it kept rising up in front of him and looking at him. What he had been hiding from himself. This was running away. He was a coward. He had played games with this child, and now he was driving away from the consequences. He passed a hand down over his forehead, pinched the bridge of his nose. Somewhere in his head, in the corner of his vision, a figure with his own eyes stood looking at him.

Usted bastardo, he told it.

But there was no choice. He started calculating the miles to the next junction. Number 19.

A minute later he reached for his phone again.

'Patz. Is me. No, listen please. Listen. I tell you something. You gonna be mad, but you save the mad for later. Yes? Stay cool. I want you just listen. Then you tell me what you think. *Si*, about three month back . . . '

Sam looked at his watch. Nearly midnight. Nearly Christmas Eve. He yawned for the hundredth time. He didn't feel well; his eyes prickled, his throat was dry, and he had the beginnings of a headache. He switched his phone on. Every few minutes throughout the long hours he had switched it on briefly. What he feared was the ringtone. If it were to ring he would have to answer it, and there would be his dad's voice, or Becky's, and they would overwhelm him. He had to just get through this bit alone. Then he would phone them.

But the phone might ring and it might be Mum.

No way. Not here. Not in this bright-lit corridor smelling of cooking fat and stale coffee, metres above an endless stream of traffic. No. It wouldn't be like that.

A text message: *Sam, ring me at home now, anytime. Please. XXX Becky.*

Soon, he said to himself. Soon I'll ring. Wait just a little longer.

Twice in the last hour a lady from behind the Ritazza

Coffee counter had come over to talk to him. Was he waiting for somebody? Where was his home? Why was he here on his own for so long, at this time of night? He had watched her reflection in the glass as she walked back between the tables, shaking her head. She and her companion had looked across to him. He knew they were discussing him.

His mobile bleeped. A second message: *Tell me where u r EXACTLY*.

He texted back.

Nothing for some minutes. Then, *You stay there. I come*.

A shiver ran down between his shoulder blades. At last, something.

What?

What was coming to him? Not Mum. A messenger . . . ? Someone who knew something?

Tony shouldered his way through the big double doors and into the broad lighted corridor of Knutsford Services, south-bound side. He surveyed the almost empty restaurant on the ground floor beside the entrance. Only a group of students, it appeared, were using the place, spreading themselves across a couple of corner tables and trying to stir up some party atmosphere with crackers and party poppers. A policeman with his cap off was chatting to one of the women at the shop counter. Tony began mounting the steps.

The small figure was still there halfway along the corridor, leaning against the rail, looking out into the night.

Tony walked up to within a few feet and stopped.

The figure stirred, turned, looked up. So: a small boy, then. A little triangular face; a bony head on a thin neck; ears bent forward, as if they were listening for something . . . and a look of what . . . ? Fear?

'You Sam?'

Sam looked at the dark stocky figure with the wild hair standing there. The man had chubby cheeks that squeezed his eyes and a bushy black moustache. Sam tried to read something in the dark eyes, but they were just resting on him, watching him. The man's arms hung loosely by his sides, the hands turned slightly outwards.

'You Sam. Yes?'

Sam nodded slowly, as if reluctant to admit it. 'Yes.'

'You looking for you mam.'

'Yes.'

'You look for long time, eh? All so many message.'

Sam noted the throaty wheeze, the breathlessness; but there was a gravelly roughness in the voice that was not unattractive.

He found himself saying, 'Did any of them reach my mum?'

Tony resisted the impulse to shrug. He looked down at the small boy. So thin. So serious. So weary.

'Who can say? You send all lots of message to me.'

Sam looked at him, thinking of all the texts he had sent. What had he pictured in his head? He could not recapture it now, that frail dream, not here in the white light of this corridor, with the endless swish of traffic passing beneath their feet, and with this squat dark man standing staring at him.

'Yes, I . . . sent all the messages. They were for my mum.

141

I was hoping my mum would read them in the Next World. I . . . I got the number of the Next World.'

Tony's eyes narrowed. 'The Nex' Wall?'

'My mum, before she died, she said to me and my sister she would be going to the Next World, and I . . . '

Tony's world slipped sideways. Then it righted itself. He studied the boy. 'Careful,' he told himself. 'You be's very careful here.'

There was a silence. Tony began to say, 'What you saying is you ma—' but he cut that short and changed it to, 'Where you live?'

'West Sheffield.'

'I live Sheffield too.' Tony clutched his chunky thighs just above each knee and bent down to the boy. 'Hey, Sam. I feeling bad. You know why? Cos I let you go on sending message to me.'

Sam looked up into the pudgy face that was now quite close to him. The eyes were dark brown like nuts; they seemed to be without mystery or hidden intentions; the flat smile looked sad.

Suddenly he knew. 'None of my messages went to Mum, did they? You don't know my mum. Why did you let me go on sending you texts?'

Tony looked at the tired face and at the weary eyes that searched his own. He closed his eyes for a moment. *Holy Mary*, he said to himself, *ayudenme. Help me here.*

'You mother,' he said slowly, 'is died. I understand this. You understand this. But also is not died . . .' Tony, eyes closed and frowning, focused on the words. It was many years since the nuns had spoken to him about these simple things. And yet, oh so not simple. 'I believe this.

But I tell you something else. Who is saying this mother is not reading you message? All the message you send. Hey? Who is say that? Not me. You know what? You send message into space. I think she read them.'

He paused. Take this easy. Don't rush. Let it come. OK, OK . . .

'Your mother is . . . ' Tony paused, waiting. Seconds ticked by. Silently he repeated the words to himself . . . until a strange and rather beautiful clarity spread itself in his brain and he saw what it was he could say to the small watchful waiting face. 'This lovely mother,' he said slowly and wonderingly, 'is waiting.'

Sam watched the eyes, which had opened for a moment to look at him and then clenched shut again. Concentrating.

'She's waiting?'

'*Si*, is waiting . . . '

Silence. Sam looked at the face; it was closed, as if it was praying. Seconds went by.

'Is waiting . . . for me . . . to . . . *take you back home*!'

Tony straightened up and eased his back. *Where had that come from?* He hadn't known what he was going to say, but then somehow the words had just come.

The small head was turned away to the window, to the streaming tail of lights; the eyes were brimming.

Tony pressed on.

'I got this idea. Because I . . . responsible. You know what I mean? You want this connection to Next World. You want connection to you mam. So, what we do—I take you home in my lorry, and . . . and maybe I help you do something about this mam you look for. Yes?'

143

Sam was not responding.

Tony consulted the map he carried in his head, saw the western edge of Sheffield and made a few quick calculations. This came automatically; he had been living for years by these mental plottings of routes and distances and times. He also looked hard at the little head on the skinny neck attached to the thin little frame in front of him.

'Please, you trust me?'

Something was swiftly draining out of Sam; the world swam and hot trickles ran down his cheeks and there was warm salt in the corners of his mouth.

'Who is at home, please?'

Sam forced himself to take a breath; but he felt himself teetering. He managed to say, 'Dad and my sister, Becky.'

'They know you here?'

Again Sam turned away. In the corner of his eye the Christmas tree in the children's corner went on flicking its lights. What had his dream been? Could any part of it survive here?

'We phone you family, then we go home?' Tony said. He turned to go back down the stairs, then paused to see if the boy would come with him.

Sam moved, uncertain. He stared back at the spot where he had stood at the wall of black glass. He felt a revisitation of all the feelings that had coloured his thoughts while he watched the headlights of cars and lorries and vans droning by beneath him. This was a place for people passing through, travelling elsewhere. Crowds of people pressed into this place for a few minutes, then left again. And other crowds of people never stopped here at all, they swept past, hurrying to be elsewhere. Sam

144

sensed this, he could feel the bleak desolation of a place where nobody ever really wanted to be. And at the same time the knowledge grew in him that his mother couldn't come to him here. She could never be here. He understood that now. Maybe she knew it too.

'Mister . . . '

Tony stopped on the third step down and turned. 'Hey, is no misters here. I am Tony. *Si?'*

Sam watched the back of Tony's curly head and the rolling motion of his back as he went down the steps ahead of him. There was writing printed across his back, but Sam wasn't reading it, he was gripping the mobile phone in his pocket. If this was how his journey ended then it was time to phone home.

He followed Tony through the concourse. He would phone outside.

The place had just a sprinkling now of weary night-travellers in it. In the Burger King section a middle-aged couple with an elderly woman were placing trays on a table; then the man headed for the toilets. Over in one corner of the restaurant a noisy group of students were having a party around a table. Tony held the door open for Sam and the two of them passed out into the cold night.

'This my lorry.'

They stood in front of the cab and Sam looked up at the black glass of the windscreen reflecting the orange lights in the lorry park. The walls of this metal beast seemed as high as a house. The huge and terrible tyres, still radiating a stink of hot rubber, were level with his head. Once or twice he had sat in lorry cabs just like this one when he had been at his dad's haulage depot.

145

Sam's cheeks stung in the cold night air. The pent-up hopes and dreams built over months had gone. All that was left now was this strange dark man and this big white lorry. And himself under the unreal orange lighting in this bleak lorry park.

He found he was shaking uncontrollably. He choked; his eyes filled with hot tears. He could not help the convulsions which shook his body.

Tony looked at the small boy crying in front of his lorry. '*Madre de Dios*,' he whispered. He squatted beside the child, and he lectured himself again: *Tony LeFanu, this one very upset child. And who to blame? Now look what you landed with. So now you deal with it*. Oddly, the voice in his head sounded like Patty. The last sentence was certainly one of the things she had said to him, among many other things, a little earlier that night.

'Sam. Sam? You listen, please. You want to go home, yes? To you ma—to you dad, and . . . and you family. So. You want a ride in this lorry? I take you?'

Sam gulped and swallowed. And swallowed. And knuckled away some of the wet from his eyes. He shook his head.

'No? You don't want? Listen. Trust me please. I-want-to-take-you-home. You know why? Is because I am to blame . . . for . . . for make you come to this place, so you think maybe you see you mam here.' In the semi-dark he squatted beside the child and tapped his own chest gently with a balled fist. 'I very sorry. What I can do? I drive you home in my lorry. I say to you dad, I explain. OK? Then I feel better. I sleep peaceful.' He ended. He had run out of ideas.

He looked into Sam's face but did not see hope or absolution there.

'. . . Is in you hands, my friend.'

Is not you who needs to sleep peaceful. Tony bowed his head.

Sam drew in a few shuddery breaths. He pulled out a handkerchief and wiped his face.

Tony sighed and turned and walked a few paces, looked out across the gleaming tarmac wasteland, the unreal sodium illumination. It was a dead time of night. Christmas Eve. *Por favor*, Tony whispered, *ayudenme!* He looked up into an empty cold sky, faintly irradiated by the floodlights. No flock of birds flickered in the upglare. The air was stone cold. Snow was forecast.

Sam looked up at the cab. He had waited so long to come to this place. He had held on to the promise, the hope, for so long. Something to bring back for Dad, and for Becky, that would make them happy. Something from Mum. I left home and came on this journey to contact Mum. Now, what's at the end of it is this worried-friendly man who talks funny and who wants to drive me home.

And at home? I'll come back in through the front door and I will have nothing.

Sam looked across at Tony standing by himself on the tarmac. He saw again the words printed on the back of his jacket. His eyes rested on them. Slowly, they sank into his mind. Then he read them: Bennett Brothers, Agricultural Contractors & Hauliers.

He swallowed. He tried to call out, but all that came was a squawk. He cleared his throat and tried again. 'Oi, mist—'

Sam walked over to him, then turned and looked down the length of the lorry, at the massive lettering printed down the side of the vehicle. BENNETT BROS HAULAGE.

'Bennett Brothers,' he said slowly, wonderingly. 'That's my dad. And my uncle Roy. They're the Bennett Brothers.'

Tony did not really hear this; he was waiting for inspiration to drop on him from the unreal glow of the night sky. He had done what he could. What more . . . ?

Then the child's words filtered through to his thoughts. He turned and saw the boy looking up at the lorry, the firm's name printed down the side.

'What you say?'

Chapter Sixteen

Constable George took a deep breath and said, 'So let me get this straight. You two were heading for London, and routing for some reason through Eyam—'

'I like to do the cross country to the M6, constable. See, we was going to stop off at my sister's in Stroud, then go on to Rickmansworth. That way we get to see the whole family.'

'A roundabout way to the big smoke, if I may say so. Anyway, you get a . . . what? . . . a feeling that all is not right . . .'

'Correct. And Darryl confirmed it. I'm psychic, Constable George. You didn't know that about me, did you? I do the circuit of the Spiritualist Churches in the Dales. I give the talk. I give out messages from the Other Side. Young Darryl here comes with me, don't you, Dazz?'

'Yeah. So, you're in Eyam in the morning, it's dough-nut time when you hear the story from your son and decide you have to come back.' Constable George took a look at his watch. 'So what kept you?'

Dazz looked down into his lap. Paul drew a tight smile.

'A bit embarrassing, that bit. Not our best day, eh, Darryl? We're up on Abney Moor, yeah? You know what it's like up there—nothing but wind and crows. The only sign of life, a gypsy horse on a chain. Thought we was being clever, didn't we, cutting across country to be quick. Only, the radiator boils. White smoke and a hot metal smell. Nasty. Plus those steep hills, and the brakes feelin' dodgy. So we stop. We waits for a lift. Nothing and nobody. I haven't got a mobile. But I focus in me mind on young Sam and I don't sense no danger or trouble around him. So I'm not over-worried on that score. Anyway, we sets off to walk. Yeah, OK, you can smile, constable, but I am a psychic, it's a gift. You can believe it or not. I hold people in me mind and I can tell if there's troubled atmosphere round them, or if they're in a calm space. Being psychic doesn't keep you from getting lost, though. To put it brief, we eventually find this farmer. Had to cross a few fields to get to his house. He come back with us to the car, we puts water into it, and he gets underneath and tightens up the brake cables. Problem sorted. What we do then is drive straight here, no stopping. Took all day, though.'

He shot a look over at Derek. 'Sorry, folks.'

Constable George glanced up at the wall clock. 'I think we'll cut this long story short. These folk have had a long evening of it so far and they'll want to rest. So you're heading to London because you're involved in a case in the High Court.' He paused, watching Paul Skinner's face. 'Expecting to go inside again, are we?'

Paul Skinner smiled.

'No, constable. We aren't. Seeing as I'm not the accused. I'm a witness this time. For the prosecution, as it happens. A little case of GBH which I happened to witness and didn't approve of. Scheduled to come up right after

Christmas, it is. So I'll have to take off again, after all this is over. But not till Mr Bennett's little lad is safe back home, I'm telling you that. Cos my Darryl here, he's involved. Though I don't hold him responsible cos he's too young, and he never really understood what this little Sam was planning, did he?'

Constable Shilling turned to Dazz. 'Any chance at all of you remembering where it was he said he was going, to meet his mum?'

Dazz shook his head. 'He just pointed to somewhere on a photocopied map.'

There was a general stirring and all four visitors rose to go. Both policemen and the Skinners, father and son, went down the path together. Derek and Becky watched them from the front door. At the gate the younger policeman turned and smiled and raised a hand.

'We'll see you in the morning. It'll get sorted, you'll see.' He looked up at the night sky. 'Feels like snow, eh?'

They watched both cars drive off into the night, leaving the street strangely quiet. There were no stars. The stillness held in it a penetrating cold.

Derek Bennett stared away down the lamp-lit avenue of the sleeping houses. Eventually, he said, 'That Skinner lad saying that Sam told him he was taking off . . . to go and meet Mum . . .' He looked at Becky standing on the cold path hunched over her folded arms. 'Remember when you told me he was playing a game, talking to Mum on her mobile . . . ? Where's he gone in his head with that idea, eh?'

Becky turned and went inside. He stood for a few moments longer in the front garden taking in the quietness of the night. Where would their Sam be if snow was to settle over Sheffield, over the land?

Tony was staring at the child who was staring at the words printed along the side of the lorry.

'What you say?'

His phone was ringing. Sam looked wonderingly at the lorry and listened to Tony's end of the conversation.

'Patz! You ain't gonna believe this . . . Sure, I got him here now. No, listen. He is name Sam Bennett . . . son of the boss, Mister Bennett . . . is true! . . . OK . . . OK . . . of course, you remember what happen, back in August . . . Mrs Bennett? *Si!* This is Mrs Bennett boy, Sam . . . is incredible, eh? . . . OK, sure . . .'

He held the phone out to Sam. 'She want to talk to you.'

Sam pressed the phone to his ear.

'Sam? Are you listening? Are you OK? Good. Now listen. You know the lady in the coffee shop in the drivers' depot? Where all the lorry drivers park at your dad's depot? Yes? You've been in the café, haven't you? You remember the lady behind the counter with the blue T-shirt? That's me, Patty LeFanu. I'm Tony's wife.'

Sam sniffed a long snaggly sniff. 'I've seen you.'

'Course you have. Now listen, Sam. Tony just told me tonight all about you and the mobile phone messages. He never knew it was you. Anyway, never mind about that now. When I stop talking to you I'm going to telephone your dad to tell him you're safe. And I'm going to suggest to him that Tony drives you home. Right now. Is that OK with you? Would you like him to do that?'

' . . . Yes.'

'Good boy.'

Tony took back the phone. 'OK, you speak to Mr Bennetts now.' To Sam he said, 'Hey, is getting cold. We go up into the cab, warm up.'

Sam had a lift up from Tony, then gripped the bars and climbed the three mountings up to the cab door with Tony's hand in his back. Tony climbed in on the other side, slid his keys into the ignition and pointed Sam to the starter button. The engine broke out into a hammering series of revs that picked up and roared. Exhaust smoke drifted off across the tarmac.

Tony waited, then pressed more buttons on his mobile. ' . . . Mr Bennetts! Is Tony! . . . Sure . . . OK . . . Yeah, is right here . . .'

The phone was passed again to Sam.

'Dad! No. I'm fine now. Dad? I'm in Tony's lorry. He's going to drive me home.'

He took in the desperation in his dad's voice as he answered a battery of questions. He was fine . . . he was safe . . . nothing bad had happened . . . he had made his way on the two trains to Knutsford . . . now he was sitting in Tony's cab, ready to begin the journey home . . . Finally his dad gave up the phone to Becky. He had to keep telling her that he was all right and he was happy now about coming home with Tony, and that she and Dad didn't have to drive over right now to fetch him.

Finally it was over. The two of them had gone on putting out reassurances until they were weary. Sam sat on the passenger seat, looked out from the height of the cab on to the lorry park. To have heard his dad's and

Becky's voices, speaking from the phone in the kitchen at home . . . it somehow made the world look different.

Tony switched on the string of coloured lights around the windscreen, and then the miniature Christmas tree.

'You like these?'

The engine roared. Warm air started to build up. Tony looked across at Sam. '*Excellente!* For first time, you smile. You ready to go home?'

Sam nodded.

Tony switched the interior lights off. 'We go.'

The monster rolled—then stopped with a jerk that almost pulled Sam off his seat.

One other person needed to be convinced that all was well.

The lady from the Ritazza Coffee counter was standing in front of the lorry with her arms folded. For the third time Tony handed his mobile over to Sam. 'Please, you phone you dad once more. Let the lady speak to him.'

Sam climbed down and Tony watched the boy speak to the lady with the white cap on her head, lead her to one side and point to the lettering printed on the lorry, offer her the phone. But she nodded and ruffled his hair and walked off back across the tarmac towards the building.

Sam climbed back up by himself.

'She said she thought you were abdicating me.'

Tony shook his head and frowned as he fed the steering wheel from one hand to the other.

They were picking up speed on the carriageway and edging into the middle lane to overtake an old small Fiat.

Tony gave a short laugh, like a bark. 'Hey, Sam. You dad, he got big surprise when he hear you is with me . . .'

154

No answer. Tony glanced across. Sam had drawn his legs up on to the seat; his head was tilted back, his face turned sideways. He was wiped out and far away, asleep with his mouth open.

Becky lay on the bed with her knees drawn up and a blanket over her, thinking. But then she must have slipped into a doze because she woke to the pounding of Dad's feet on the stairs; then she heard the telephone ringing. The green numbers on her night clock showed five past one. She was belting a towelling robe around her on the stairs when Dad, out of sight below, shouted, 'Patty!' She sank on to the top stair, hunched over her knees. Between his listening silences she heard him say, 'Where? . . . Tony? . . . I don't believe it . . .' Then there was a long period while Dad listened, only occasionally saying quietly, 'Good God . . . He didn't, did he?'

She couldn't make a picture out of what she was hearing, but the tone of her dad's voice was reassuring. He was coming to the end of the conversation, saying, 'Yes,' and 'Fine, I'll do that,' and jotting things on a pad. Eventually he put the phone down and stood there looking up the stairs at her.

'That was Patty LeFanu. You know, the woman who runs our café at the depot? Sam went to Knutsford Services on the M6 Motorway, south of Manchester. Now he's on his way home in her husband's lorry. He's one of our drivers, Tony LeFanu. He's driving him home.'

'In the lorry?'

'Says he'll bring him here, to the door.'

Becky and her dad stared at each other.

'He went by himself to Knutsford Motorway Services,' Derek said quietly. He turned back to the phone and pressed numbers.

Becky closed her eyes. 'Thank God.' She had never ever felt such a depth of relief. She found a tissue in the pocket of the robe and pressed it against her eyes.

She listened to her dad talking, first to Tony, then to Sam, and she cried in complete silence. By the time Dad passed her the phone she had her voice under control.

The engine shuddered and died away. Sam woke to strange silence. He found he was lying on top of a duvet on the sleeping shelf immediately behind the driving cab. The curtains that normally screened this compartment were tied back. He lifted his head and looked at Tony's tangled hair silhouetted against a pale light. Tony sensed the stir behind him.

'Hey, Sam. You OK? You want some coffee? I got a stove here.'

Sam swung his legs off the bunk and climbed back into the passenger seat. He rubbed his eyes and yawned. They both stared at the early pearling of dawn-light outside. They were in a narrow passing place in a narrow lane in a narrow valley that was utterly still and silent and cast in crystalline white. Tony switched the headlights back on for a few moments and Sam stared at a glittering tangle of dead bracken and old grasses encrusted in ice crystals.

'Hey, Sam, while you sleeping I get big troubles with the roads. We come many long ways around. First is this road shut, then is that one. Is bad weathers in the hills. The radio say snow. Is not so easy with this lorry. So. We stop here for a minute. Make some coffee. Ah . . . 'Scuse. Gotta go outside.'

'Me too.'

Sam pulled his hoodie on and Tony helped him down onto the ground and they went off to relieve themselves at different ends of the lorry. There was an iron-cold in the air. Sam looked down the slope across white fields to the lumpy side of a hill that rose up and up to a treeless ridge. In the steal of early light there was an eerie silence over the frozen valley. Heavy white-grey cloud seemed to restrict the light. He looked down onto old tussocks of long grass that covered a sloping bank up to a fence. The grass was tangled and broken into angles and rigid with a glitter of frost. It crackled when Sam stood on it. His breath smoked and hung in a cloud in the air. He looked about while he peed and a cloud of steam rose from the ground. There was a shuffle of movement in the field beyond the fence where a jostle of sheep had edged forward to look at him. Their breath steamed about their heads, and one or two of them stamped the rigid ground. Behind him the hot lorry ticked and creaked in the cold air.

Something small and fine tickled the back of his neck. And there was a featherlight touch on his hair. He looked up. Suddenly and without warning the world had filled with sinking snowflakes. Millions of them were floating down in complete silence. White tufts of featherdown. They streaked his cheeks and brushed the tip of his nose, and they lay on his sleeves. One caught on his eyelashes and blurred things. He turned to look around: the valley had disappeared behind a thickening curtain of falling snowflakes.

Before he climbed back up into the cab he stopped to listen. The snow was making a very faint sound as it fell and settled. *Whisp*. Half a whisper.

That trickling-light touch of the snowflake on his neck had reminded him of something—something he wanted to remember. What was it?

Before they got back into the cab Tony showed Sam his joke. He held up a card against the rear of the lorry. *How's my driving? Crap! Phone 999*.

'Hey, you don't tell the boss, eh?'

They sat in the warm cab and watched the big flakes settling onto the window and melting and sliding down the glass.

'Is beautiful, eh?' Tony switched on his Christmas lights and then poured water from a plastic bottle into a pan and set it on a paraffin stove. The coffee was hot and sweet; they dipped biscuits into it. Tony wound down his window.

'Hey. You hear?'

From somewhere down in the frozen valley there came the thin bubbling call of a bird.

'Tony, when will we get back home?'

'OK, we see . . . Right now, we not so far from Sheffield South. So, I say later this morning? Is OK for you?' He slurped his steaming coffee and then shook out a cigarette from a crumpled pack on the dashboard. 'Provide the snow don't get too deep.' The window was still wound down; he blew a plume of smoke out among the snowflakes. 'You want to tell how you get from you house to that place, Knutsford? You hitch? Like this?'

Sam shook his head at the stubby thumb.

'I got on to two trains.'

'Is true? Very good. And you do this after all the tex' message because you think you mam is reading the words . . . ?'

Sam said, 'I think my mum knows I'm here.'

'You know, I hear about you mam. I hear the boss Mr Bennett lose his wife sudden. I talk to her one time on the telephone, but I never see her. So. You tell me about her?'

Sam sipped his coffee. He spoke haltingly at first, but then more fluently, about Mum in her own classroom where she taught at school, Mum getting the very bad headaches, Mum seeing the doctor and then being admitted to the hospital. Then Mum at the hospice, Saint Luke's. The last place he had seen her.

Tony threw his cigarette stub out of the window. 'So. Is time we move. This snow come thick, eh.'

They drove slowly down the narrow lane, negotiating bends and junctions, running alongside cold black woodland, high moor skylines, and bracken and heather slopes, and high eruptions of grey boulder-stone littering the hillsides—all of it taking a capping of snow. Tony said they were cutting across country, coming in to Sheffield's south side. He said it was OK to drive his lorry through this country because there would be little traffic at this time of day.

Sam slept.

When he woke again it was still snowing, and they were driving past people's houses and he could see again, as on his train journey, snapshots of other families'

Christmases, cosy decorated interiors, domestic scenes in kitchens and living rooms where people were trying to live and be happy with each other. There were children outside in gardens and parks, playing in the snow. He felt well rested this time. It was Christmas Eve. And he was hungry.

Tony started talking. 'When I was small kid, like you, I live in Spain. I live near the sea, near the mountains. Very lucky boy. I live with my mother in this small village. This very small village on the side of the mountains, with the hills all cover for miles and miles with this trees. Pine trees. Beautiful pine trees. Very very black, tall, very straight. Like this English church steeple. You know? I spend many times in this woods, hunting, building camp. In this forest there is big deep silence. So you don't shout. You don't talk when you there. When you in this wood you whisper. So. My dad one day he is gone. He drive away. I never see him no more. I live with my mam. But I go hunting in this mountains, in this forest.' He paused and glanced across at Sam.

'Then, when I eight years old . . .' Tony waited.

'Did she die?'

Tony gave a shout. 'Ha. You think! No. My mother is still live in Spain. She is seventy-seven year in same village. No, when I eight years old my *grand*mother—you follow?—she say to me "Tony, you the only boy likes to play in the forest. No one else play alone there."'

Sam watched Tony sitting bent slightly forward, his arms resting on the steering wheel. From this angle his moustache seemed to sprout out like a little straggly dark hedge, and his cheekbones almost hid his eyes. He shot Sam a quick glance. 'Is maybe just because I like

160

this peaceful silence. Is like when you put you ear to the well, you know? And you listen, like this. So. Is maybe why I drive this lorries.'

'Why did my message to Mum go to you?'

Tony looked at him. 'I dunno. Why?'

'I saw a telephone number in Mum's writing. It looked like "Contact number . . . " and there was a telephone number. So I thought it was—'

'Ha!' Tony slapped his thigh. 'Is me! I phone you house one time. I leave message for you dad about some delivery problem, I dunno, I forget. But you mam take the message. Is Contact Me! My mobile!' Tony hooted. 'All the time you send one message and then another message—to me. All this times, you think is getting through to you mam? You hope? Because you think this the number of the Nex' Worl'? And even if is Tony, you thinking I maybe passing the message on, huh?'

'Yes.'

They drove in silence, absorbing this little piece of knowledge.

Eventually Tony said, 'So what is the message? What is the message for you mam?'

Sam was silent for a few moments. 'I . . .' He hesitated. What *was* his message? What was her message to him?

'Mum used to lie in a hospital bed and she wore a big floppy woollen hat on her head and it covered all the side of her face because she had a tumour growing in her brain and she said she didn't want us to remember her with an ugly face and she said we were going to be sad but all the time we had to remember—that's Becky my sister and me—we had to remember that she was still going to be herself somewhere, *she* wasn't going to die, only her body was, so I thought of her in that somewhere place and I kept sending her messages from me to show I still remembered her as she was—'

'And all the time you sending to me, in the Nex' Worl'! Is me! I am the Nex' Worl'. Tony LeFanu is Paradiso! I tell that one to Patz.' He smiled across to Sam, a fat, creased smile. 'You see my wife, called Patz, in the depot café? She don't always think she in Heaven when she with me. She gonna give me hell when I get home. She—what they say?—one fightsy woman.'

Sam pondered this for a moment.

'My sister says a word like that, but she says feisty.'

'Sure. Is what I say. Fightsy. Anyways, you know why I keep the contact with you all these time? You know why?' Tony tapped his chest gently with a fist. 'Is because I feel in my heart you story. This one upset kid, I say. What I can do? So I let you keep sending message. I want to know why you calling for Mam all these time.' He paused. Then he added, 'Also, I am sorry for what happen to you.'

Sam looked at Tony and let the fact sink in that this man had been receiving all his texts, had held in his hand so many small questions, so many little groups of words that he had imagined his mum reading, or knowing about. He watched Tony's hands gripping the wheel, his arms trembling slightly with the vibration.

He wished that Driscoll and Geordie could be there at his house when he drew up to the kerb.

'So, in the summer you mam, she die. In the hospital.'

Sam nodded. 'In Saint Luke's.'

'And there is service. For her? All you friends come?'

Sam nodded again. 'At the Crematorium.'

'Sam, excuse please, but that is one big bloody horrible word, eh?'

Sam smiled.

'And then. What happen then? Dad, sister, you, all back home. No Mam.' He paused. 'So you begin to ask question—where is all dead people go? No answer. Yes?'

Sam said nothing, watching him.

'Me too. You know, I sometime ask this questions. But you. You send this question out into air. And it land on me.'

Sam suddenly remembered what it had felt like to be texting his mum with all that bottled-up hope. For some reason he thought of the greenhouse at the end of their garden. It was always warm in there, and it had an earthy comforting green-sap scent of tomato plants.

It was still early, but there was some traffic appearing now. The roads were white, the gardens were white, the rooftops were white, and the cab window was driving into an endless whirl of white flakes. Tony slowed and steered the lorry around a roundabout and off it towards the city centre.

Tony scratched his stubbly chin. He said slowly, 'On this way to you home, I think we stop a couple places.' He shot a quick glance at Sam. 'Or maybe is you take me.'

There was almost no traffic in the city, just an occasional slow car gingerly steering in low gear along the snow-filled roads. Sam watched this small but heavy dark man beside him controlling this enormous vehicle, driving it through Sheffield City Centre. He looked out of the window at passing roads and recognized skylines, tower blocks. The City Hall.

Then they were in Glossop Road, and the lorry sighed to a halt with the engine battering rhythmically. Sam edged to the front of his seat, grasped the dashboard shelf and peered out at the grey cliff-face and all the angled windows of the Royal Hallamshire Hospital.

'Is where you mam was. Yes?'

'She was up in there. In one of the rooms.'

'So, you visit, you go into this place many many time.'

'Yes. Then after a while she moved to the hospice.'

'It was quick, eh, this tumour? So, you see Mam there in the bed. You sit by the bed. She talk to you about this dying?'

'Yes. She had a bandage around her head, then later it was a hat. Like this.' Sam covered one eye with a slanting hand.

Cars coming out of the hospital car park were pausing and the drivers were peering up at them before driving out through the gates. There were a few tentative hoots from behind. Tony ignored them.

'So. Go on. You tell. She grow bad with this tumour.'

'They moved Mum into a small room by herself.'

'And you go, you sit also in this room. What you do? You like to read to you mam? Play game?'

Sam nodded.

'Go on. Tell what happen.'

Cars were hooting regularly now. One by one they edged out and drove around them. A green and white chequered ambulance nosed out into Glossop Road.

'She didn't sit up any more. We didn't stay long. She was sleeping.'

'You hold her? You touch her?'

164

'Yes.'

'Go on. You tell.' Tony looked at him, his eyes were almost fierce.

'I held her hand. I . . . when she was sleeping nearly all the time . . . Dad let me climb up on the bed. I think it was the last time. She had her hand on my head.'

'She say?'

Sam said nothing. There was a long silence. Something was engulfing him, dissolving him.

He swallowed. ' . . . She said, I love you . . . Don't be afraid . . . She said, I'm not going far away.'

'Go on.'

'She was sleeping.'

'So. She sleeping.'

'She didn't talk any more. She went into a long sleep.'

'You are there . . . when . . . ?'

'She died while she was sleeping. She died at two o'clock in the morning. My dad told me that. I was there until late, I don't know what time it was, but I went home with Auntie Pam. I think Dad and Becky went back to the hospital, I don't remember, all I remember is Dad coming into my bedroom very early in the morning and he sat on my bed and said that Mum had gone. He said it was like first she had slipped away off into sleep, and then she had slipped away further to somewhere else, somewhere further off than sleep.'

Snow had been settling on the windscreen, building up in an uneven ledge. Tony stared through the glass. Scurries of wind were swirling the snowflakes up into the air, but the relentless falling of large flakes went on uninterrupted. He left the silence in the cab untouched.

'You got hanky?' Tony looked away out of the cab window at the hospital buildings. Here and there resting on the sills of the windows were just visible some small signs that human beings were there in the rooms behind the glass: an off-centre vase of flowers, a coloured soft toy, a piece of paper sellotaped to the glass, a little stack of books or magazines. Wisps of steam were drifting away off the top of a white chimney on a flat-topped roof.

'So. We go to this hospice now. Saint Looks. You know where?'

Tony made the lorry hiss and he revved the engine. They rolled.

Ecclesall Road, with barely any traffic on it. Gardens filling up with snow. Houses with thick snow on their roofs, and black trees holding up white shelves of snow. Abbey Road, a broad unmarked avenue of pure white . . . Common Lane. Tony peered up the narrow road between the cottagey houses. 'Holy Moly, I got to take this thing up there?'

They wheezed and squeezed and edged between parked cars and garden gates, turned a bend and there among the snow-laden trees were the low brick buildings of the hospice. There was a small car park, but Tony drew to a halt in the road.

'This the place?'

Sam nodded. They looked across to the broad glass doors that led into a reception area. A woman was visible behind a counter. Nearby they could see a group of low tables and armchairs.

So familiar.

'How long she was here?'

'I think it was two weeks.'

Snow went on falling. Tony turned the engine off.

Silence.

'You mam is religious person?'

'No. She said she was a free spirit.'

'What is free spirit?'

'I asked her that. She said she wanted to stay free to fly about, like an angel.'

'Not like Angel of the North, eh?'

They smiled at each other.

'You remember what she say to you?'

Sam looked over the roof in the direction of his mother's room.

Her room.

He saw her hair squashed against the crisp linen of her pillow, her hand lying on the sheet, the wedding ring, the funny lop-sided beret, her half-smile, her one kind eye.

Tony waited. Occasionally someone went in or came out through the entrance doors. A car pulled up, parked, and a family walked inside balancing a small tower of wrapped presents.

'Peoples die. Everybody. For life to be life, you got also to have the death. Is true? Easy to say. But we talking here about . . . you mother.'

Tony watched the snow filling up the spaces between things outside. The world was gradually assuming a uniform shape of huge smooth white forms. If he didn't move from here soon it might be difficult to use the roads. And it was time they telephoned the boy's home again. And he was feeling pretty hungry. And—

There was a knock on the door on Sam's side of the cab.

Chapter Seventeen

The bang was on the cab door beside Sam. Someone had climbed up the footings and was knocking. There was a muffled call: 'Sam! Sam Bennett!'

Sam buzzed his window down. 'Melanie!'

A face bobbed up outside. It was a young thin face with enormous eyes and an open mouth with irregular teeth. The straight blonde hair was pulled up into topknots on either side of the head, two short splay-fountains. She wore tinsel earrings.

'What are you doing in this enormous—oooh, hello? Are you the driver?' An arm and a hand was thrust through the window. 'I'm Melanie.' Tony leaned across to shake it.

'*Si*. Yes, is my lorry.'

Sam said, 'This is Tony.'

'Isn't this snow great? Here, have you come for the party? Come on. They'll all love to see you.' She opened the door and pulled Sam's sleeve. 'Come on.' He climbed down after her and jumped off the last footing into a depth of powder. She held his hand and they ran across to the entrance doors, his shoes making soft shuddery noises in the snow.

It was Melanie. Melanie who had curled Mum's hair; who had sat beside the bed and done things to Mum's fingernails with her set of tiny tools, chatting all the while; Melanie the beautician, Melanie the terrible gossip, goofy Melanie who knew everyone in St Luke's Hospice.

Four months had gone by, but it might have been four minutes. He went in through the doors and the same smell was in the air; the same pictures were on the walls; there was the same smart carpet, and the arrangement of chairs and low tables opposite the Reception Desk. He knew the woman behind the counter and she gave him a cheery wave, but they couldn't really speak because of the noise coming from the lounge. Music, and a mingle of many voices talking over each other. Melanie pulled him straight into it, and over the noise called out, 'Look, everyone, Sam's come back to visit us.'

He looked at the grey-faced, hollow-cheeked patients in dressings gowns; and those who were dressed in their own clothes but sitting lightly on the edge of their chairs, as though they might be called to get up and leave at any moment; and the family visitors, Mums, Dads, children; and the staff who were busy handing round teas and crackers and plates of cakes and biscuits. Somebody put a cup of tea into his hand. Sam looked at plates of sausage rolls and mince pies and biscuits that stood on low tables and realized how hungry he was. He looked across at the aquarium and recognized the same fish that he always thought looked like a small flat plate painted in luminous candy-stripes still wagging its way back and forth in front of the glass as it had done all those weeks ago, when Mum was still alive. Mum still Mum. Here, in a room down the corridor.

Several people whose faces he remembered came up and said hello, said how nice it was he had dropped in on their party—and where was his sister and his dad? He was trying to explain this when Melanie reappeared.

'I've been trying to get your friend to come in, but he won't. I think he's just shy.' She plucked his sleeve. 'Here, come and sit down for a minute and tell me what's going on. Why isn't your dad here, and what's with you and this lorry?'

He gave her his tea to hold. 'One minute.'

He plodded through the snow round to Tony's side of the cab. He looked up at the dark silhouette behind the window. Tony was busy talking on the phone.

The window buzzed down. 'Sure . . . I do that . . . is here now . . . OK . . . is no problem . . . sure.'

He pressed a button on his mobile, leaned forward to crush out his cigarette, and climbed down. 'OK. I come. I speak with you dad. You ring him now from this place. I speak with Patz . . . ay ay ay.' He shook his head. Then he looked at Sam. 'Maybe you come to my house with me. She not be so on fire if you with me.'

They paused under some of the trees and their snow-blanketed branches. Tony squinted up. 'Is like cake, eh?' Their voices sounded enclosed, as if enfolded in a white room. He looked at Sam. 'Who is Melanie?'

Sam tried to remember all the things he knew about her. The way she made the nurses laugh; her funny stories to Mum about going shopping with her boyfriends; her wacky clothes.

'She's not a nurse. She is a sort of volunteer here. She works with the patients. She's a beauty person. She does Indian head massage. And she does their hair and their nails and she does make-up on them. She's funny.'

He used the phone at the Reception Desk.

He spoke to Becky first and described some parts of his strange day. She sounded peeved. 'Sam, you're such a doofus. Dad and I are just sitting around here at home with all this snow piled up outside so we can't go anywhere, and you're out there having a wild time.' But she blew him a kiss down the line.

His dad was more guarded, anxious for details. 'Sam. You're at Saint Luke's. With Tony, right? What are you— Why did you—What's that noise?'

'It's a party, Dad. Everybody's really pleased to see me. They wish you and Becky were here too.'

'Tell them we'd come if we could, but we're snowed-in. Some of the roads around here are blocked by abandoned cars. Anyway, I've talked to Tony. He'll drop you as near here as he can, we'll meet you if he can't get down these roads, then he'll drive on to the depot.'

Melanie took over the phone for a few moments.

While he watched her and listened to her reassurances, Sam felt a small surge of relief, joy almost. His dad wasn't angry. And when he got back home, things would be all right.

Someone was playing a CD of jazzed-up carols loudly in the lounge. Over the noise, Sam told Melanie the story of his meeting with Tony, how they had parked in the road and looked again at the hospital. Then they had driven here.

She looked at him now, her eyes roaming his face for a few seconds. 'Your dad was worried. He had to tell the police you'd gone missing, in case something bad had happened to you.'

171

Sam raised his eyes from the carpet.

'Will I be in trouble?'

'No. He's told them where you are, so they can stop looking.' She smiled at him, one of her wide smiles that showed all her funny teeth.

'So, this Tony's taken you to the Hallamshire, and now he's brought you here.' She looked away, thinking. 'Would you like to go and have a look at your mum's room?'

She got up and went to one of the women sitting in the lounge. Sam looked at the party. There were shouts and hoots of laughter above the music. Tony standing talking to people beside a huge plant with dark green shiny leaves. He was pretending to dance a little from side to side to the music.

He went with Melanie along the broad hall-corridor, branched off into another section, passed through some doors into a second hall . . . and there was the door.

Always on all the visits Mum had been behind this door, lying there in her bed.

The bed was neatly made, but on the side table now there were pink-framed reading glasses, two paperbacks, a Walkman, a bottle of lemon barley water, small pill bottles, tissues, and a Christmas flower arrangement of brilliant red leaves mixed up with gold-sprayed pods . . . Someone else was here now, but she was sitting in the lounge and she had said she didn't mind them going in. There was the same picture on the wall: a woodland path with bluebells in spring. Sam walked across to the big window and looked at the view over the gardens. The garden under the silent rain of snowflakes was unrecognizable now, a sculpture park of thickened white shapes.

The light was greying; this winter day would soon be fading out into dusk. It seemed incredible that back in August he had walked on the lawns in the sun, and beyond under the shady trees.

He turned back to the bed. Mum had lain there. He had crawled up onto this very bed and put his weight gently beside her legs. He had rested his head under her arm, and her hands had moved on his neck and on the back of his head, and her stroking fingers had been so light. Like . . . He remembered something now. Hours ago at dawn he had stood in the freezing stillness of the country lane in a world rigid and whitened in frost crystals, and something had touched his hair, the back of his neck. The first snowflakes. He had not recognized it then. But it had been just like the last touch of his mother's fingers.

He turned, but found he was alone in the room. Melanie had slipped out. He looked at the wall above the bed, the chair in the corner. Spaces between things.

Mum. Alice Bennett, in this space. He took his mobile phone out of his pocket and looked at it, then put it away. Outside it was snowing again, large flakes sailing down in silence, muffling the world.

There was death. The real fact of it. And it was not a separate and dread thing; it was a fact, like the snow outside. If you could look straight at the world and everything that it contained, then you also looked at death, because the world and death are not separate. But some things don't die. I love Mum. I love her now, at this moment. And I know absolutely that she loves me. That does not die.

* * *

173

He walked back along the corridor alone. When he got back to the lounge the party had moved on to Christmas pop songs. Melanie was dancing with Tony beside the aquarium. The candy-striped fish still flipped itself up and down lengths of the tank in front of a stream of bubbles and yellow-green weed. Most of the people in the lounge were wearing paper hats, and a huge plate of Christmas cake was being passed around. Sam's phone buzzed in his pocket. It was Patty LeFanu. He started to talk but she interrupted:

'It's Patty, Sam. Not Mrs Leaf Anew, OK? Listen, what's that mad husband of mine doing?'

Sam looked at Tony's bottom wagging from side to side. Both his arms were held out wide, as if he were ready to hug someone, but in his hands there were a mince pie and a sausage roll.

'He's . . . um, having a cup of tea and a mince pie and he's making some of the nurses laugh.'

'Yup. That sounds about right.'

'Mrs Leff—Patty? He said you're cross with him. Please don't be cross. He's . . . he's . . . ' Sam hesitated. What could he say? What had Tony done? 'He helped me. Really. He's . . . he's taking me home.'

There was a silence.

Then, 'Yes. That's my husband. He has a heart in him, that man. It's why I married him. He doesn't always get things right, though. He gets weird ideas. You know what he told me he wants—'

But Sam was holding the phone out to Tony.

* * *

Outside at the edge of the snow they paused.

'Nice place. Nice peoples,' Tony said.

Melanie blew a cloud of breath out into the air. 'The best.'

'All those peoples there—they gonna die?'

They were arm-in-arm under the entrance roof. Sam stood with them, looking out across the white world at the lorry. Melanie's party hat sat askew across her forehead; she screwed her nose up at Tony. 'Yeah, I guess so. There's no getting away from that one. Sooner or later. But it's not what this place is about, Tony love. You see, what I do . . . I make them look good, and that helps them feel good. So then they're set up for doing the living now.'

'Sure.'

'I'm not one for reading heavy stuff, but I saw something the other day, made me think about what we do here. It was Doctor Johnson. He said that when a person knows they're gonna be executed in the morning it concentrates the mind, big time. See, to me that means when you know death's coming you can stop living in some hopeful future, which never exists anyway, and you can start living here and now, in the present. That's what Saint Luke's is about. Making the best of now.'

Tony frowned. 'He work here?'

'Who?'

'This Doc Johnson.'

'Er . . . no. He's dead.'

Tony blew out his cheeks at the cold air. 'Too bad. We gotta go. Hey, when I get sick, I come to this place. OK? You be here?'

'Tony, if you come I'll give you the pedicure, the manicure—the full treatment: I'll make you beautiful.'

175

'Maybe just the cure, eh?'

Mel slung her arm around Sam's neck and high-stepped with him through the snow to the lorry. She raised her face to the dallying snowflakes, beaming. 'Isn't this just so amazing? When have we ever had a Christmas Eve like this?'

'I'm going home now,' said Sam, 'to Dad and Becky.'

'Give 'em my love. Here, Tony's a honey, isn't he? Is he married?'

Sam nodded down to her from the top step beside the open door of the cab. 'To my dad's café manager at the depot. Mrs Lef—Patty.'

Melanie did a little mad dance in front of the cab, threw a snowball, and blew them both a kiss, then she scurried back across the snow to join the small group that was sheltering in a huddle at the entrance. Tony started the engine. They waved. There were inaudible calls from the group. The enormous vehicle rolled backwards, reversed into a goods delivery entrance, then slowly edged forward. The lorry tooted.

They drove slowly back along Common Lane between little gates and front gardens, pavements and low walls.

A white world. Snow still fell in big flakes, but at a slower and more spaced-out pace than earlier in the day. Nothing moved on the roads. But people were about, muffled in scarves and hats, rolling-up snowmen, throwing snowballs, sliding.

Tony was screwing up his eyes against the white glare, which reduced them to slits. He still wore his yellow paper hat from a cracker perched on his black hair.

'Hey, you wanna phone Mr Bennetts, say we back on the road, we on the way.'

They turned left out of Abbey Road back into the Ecclesall Road. Tony drove slowly. He held the steering wheel lightly with his fingers on the underside, as if feeling through to the wheels and their grip on the road.

Sam spoke again to his dad, then switched off. 'Dad says don't go on if you start sliding.'

Tony humphed. 'Of course. Who is lorry driver here? Is very many tonnes we sitting on. When this wheels don't grip, eh? . . . is when we stop. Walk home—*Ah!*' His mouth tightened. 'Ay, ay, ay . . . ' He dug a hand into the softness of his belly and pushed it around for a few moments. 'Got aches in the gut.'

The police roadblock was three minutes up the road. Two blue and green chequered Vauxhalls, their blue roof-lights flickering, were parked bonnet-to-bonnet across the avenue. Four policemen in Day-Glo jackets stood in the road.

Tony ground to a halt and buzzed the window down.

A policeman walked over. 'It's no go along here, mate. We've got abandoned vehicles, a jack-knifed artic. There's nothing going further up this road for a while. Hallam Moor Edge? Your best bet is to take a right here and try and come around from the moorside. Can't promise you'll make it, though. You sure you got to do this?'

Tony was leaning out of the window and speaking downward so Sam heard no more than a mutter. He revved the engine, released the brakes, and spun the wheel.

The new road climbed a gentle slope and soon opened out on the left into fields, pastures, and stretches of open moorland, all of it blanketed in a thickness of snow that rounded up every hedge, fence-post, shed, and logpile into simple lumpish shapes.

The day was beginning to die. The snow was taking on a grey light.

'OK, so now we phone the dad again. We tell what we do.'

It was Becky who answered. 'Good-oh, Sam. You nearly here? It's Christmas Eve, you know. Stop joy-riding in that lorry and get back here.' She sounded bouncy. 'You want to know what's happening here? Dad is trying to wrap his presents. You know how good he is at that. And I'm in the kitchen helping Auntie Pam. We're doing stuff for Christmas dinner tomorrow. And Uncle Roy is round at Mrs Prythurch's trying to get her to come to dinner with us. And guess what, Dad's invited that Dazz and his dad to come too . . . '

She paused while Sam told her about the detour.

'OK, I'll tell Dad. But you tell Tony to put foot. I might go to Midnight Mass with my friends, so get back before—' The phone cut out. Sam held out the phone to Tony.

'Is maybe too much snow. On the mast. Cut signal.'

Tony's breathing sawed in his throat, and his eyes were screwed up. From time to time he would dig a hand in his belly. He glanced across to Sam. 'Is OK. Don't worries. Got a bit sick feeling, is all.'

They had left residential houses behind. Here were small-holdings, isolated farms, sheep fields, and stone barns. In one field a man had left his tractor with its lights burning out over the snow and was shaking out a bale of hay among sheep. They passed a farm where the cows

178

were gathered by a gate in a quagmire of mud and slushy snow waiting to be let into the yard to be milked.

They turned into a narrow road that seemed to head straight out on to the moors, except that featureless acres of blanketing whiteness now surrounded them. 'This way take us round . . . *Aaah* . . . ' Tony was gasping and blowing. Sam watched the unblemished surface of snow passing under their bonnet; but he also kept slipping looks across at Tony who was wheezing noisily. Every other breath was a gasp.

They switched on the headlights. Snowflakes continued to slant down in their crowded multitudes across the beams and occasionally a flurry of smoky powder blew off a hedge across their path. Tony groaned suddenly.

'Tony? What's the matter? Are you sick?'

He didn't answer. Presently the lorry slowed and Tony pulled the wheel so that they drew up in a passing place. The ground rose ahead in two dark humps on either side of the road. For a moment he sat panting, then he reached and switched off the engine.

'Tony?'

He was gripping and twisting the flesh of his stomach. Every intake of breath was snatched; every exhalation a shudder. He looked at Sam. '*Virgen Santisima, ayudame a salir de esta, te lo pido por mis hijos* . . . Sorry . . . not feel so good.' He lifted his hands and looked at them. 'What wrong with these? Got prickling, pins and needles. Got some pains here.' He dug and squirmed the heel of his hand into his ribs, as if he could grind something away.

Sam stared at Tony. He was making blowing noises through his moustache and his dark eyes weren't

179

seeing; they were preoccupied with the pain. Sam got off his seat and leaned over to look into Tony's face. He was very white, and his eyes stared back at Sam. They looked scared.

'*No puedo continuar asi . . . me voy a desmayar . . . Voy a vomitar*. Sam, sorry . . . it don't look like I drive you this last bit . . . sorry, I wanted to drive you to house . . . maybe you get someone . . . ' He dropped his head back against the seat. He closed his eyes, panting through bared teeth.

Sam sat still. He listened. This had been a quiet road, there were no other cars. The little Christmas tree on the dashboard glowed its tiny pyramid of red and green and orange and yellow; and all around the windscreen the coloured bulbs burned their fierce little colours.

Silence. But for the terrible noise of Tony catching at breaths. The cab was turning into a darkening cave as snow built up on the stilled wipers and climbed steadily up the glass.

Tony's eyes were closed. His face was grey-white.

Sam tried the mobile. There was no signal.

Tony gasped and groaned.

Sam's mind leapt. Climb down and run along the road—which way?—for help? Or stay with Tony?

'*Dios.*'

'Tony? Can you hear me? I'm going to find someone to help you. Don't worry, please. Tony?'

It seemed that Tony nodded. His teeth were bared, his breathing sawed in his throat.

Sam opened the door on to a cold black world filled with loose feather-light stuff that caught in his eyelashes

180

and eyebrows and left ice-touches on his lips. He climbed down, slammed the door above him, then jumped.

The lorry's red tail-lights glowed in the dark-white world like jewels. He could see the outline of the road between fences and hedges. He pulled his hood up, set his head down against the drive of the snow, shoved his hands into his pockets, and set his body to a rhythm of plodding, with each step notching further down into the compressed depth. Everywhere were the pale layers of lying snow, but darkened air had closed in, air filled with dropping flakes. He could taste the momentary fluff on the lips, taste a needle of ice, then it was gone. What had happened to Tony was frightening. Tony had been in control of everything. Tony was taking him home. Now his face had turned a terrible white and his eyes were closed and he was groaning, and once or twice his arms had jerked and flailed. Sam had drawn his legs up on to the seat when that happened, when it seemed that Tony was out of reach, out of hearing.

He stopped and peered ahead for lights, a farmhouse, a road, but he could see nothing. He looked behind. The red glow of the lorry's tail-lights had disappeared in a blackness busy with falling particles. He drove his legs on along the level that he still took to be the road. There had been fence posts and the dark loom of a hedge beside him, but these seemed to have gone now. Soon he would see the lights of a house.

He did not know how long he walked, but he thought of Dad and Becky at home watching through the windows for the big headlights, listening for the huge growl of the big engine. How long would they wait? They would do something about looking for him, wouldn't they? When? And now it was so dark. How far back down the road was Tony? Was he still gasping and wheezing? Was he going to die alone in his cab while Sam trudged in snowy darkness?

He stopped; turned round. No lights anywhere in the dark. A black world. Silence. But a silence that whispered all around him. Feather-light snowflakes clung to his eyebrows and eyelashes and tickled his cheeks. Should he turn back? Which way *was* back? Where was the road now? He lifted his feet and pressed a few more footholes in the snow, then stopped again. It was so dark; and the air of this dark night was filled with falling snow. Was he still going forward along the road? He looked up and scanned the black floating space all around him; he was seized by a sudden ballooning disorientation. A call escaped from his throat: '*Where*—?'

He stood still, and the darkness went on falling about his head.

'Oh, God!'

He dared not move. Not one step in any direction. He stood immobile, staring into a night that busied itself all about him in flurries and in sweeping silences. There was no way back. And there was no way forward. He had come to the end. Snow thickened on his arms; he could not feel his toes any more. He had thought he was setting out to touch his mum again, to look into her eyes again, feel her love touch him and warm him again. But he had lost her. And then Tony had brought reassurance, and more. He had revisited the places where she had gone from him; he had felt how it would be, letting her go . . .

And now. He was beyond all that.

He stood staring in the black that seemed to suck his thoughts away. There was no reflecting face this time. Why could he not move on, fight his way forward, find a distant light, find help? Why had all directions vanished in this lightless night?

I've come to an end. What is here? Nothing.

He remembered standing in Mum's room at the hospice, standing by the bed near to where someone else's glasses were neatly folded, and someone else's barley water stood. Mum was lying there, in that bed. And then he was lying there with her. He dozed and dreamed there. And then someone said something.

He remembered now. Someone had said, 'It's time to go.'

Who said it? Dad? Mum? A nurse? Did he imagine it?

'It's time to go now.'

He had heard it before, often in his life. At the end of a party. Nice words. They usually meant you were going home.

Why did they come back to him now? Was somebody saying, This is enough? Time to go home now?

He had closed his eyes anyway, closed his eyes and felt himself falling into the reeling night, but when he opened them again he wasn't falling, so that when the busy lights, so fierce, so piercing, blue and white, drew nearer and nearer, drew right up close, darting their splinters of white and blue mirrors into his eyes, he threw up his arms at them and cried at them, and when they halted in front of him so that their shafts, their beams and their radiance illuminated the world of flying particles and the tall dark figures moved blackly in front of the lights and then surrounded him, he cried out again—and reached out to touch them.

The last thing he felt were the huge arms that this time caught him as he fell.

Chapter Eighteen

'Sam. Sam!'

The face that may or may not have looked a bit like Mum resolved itself into Becky's face. He looked up into it through a haze of sleep. Then he had a mouthful of hair pressed against him as Becky buried her face in his neck. He lay still and looked up at his bedroom ceiling and let her squeeze him. Then he closed his eyes. Some time later he felt her lift her head away and look down at him.

'You were shouting. You were calling out, something about falling into a canyon. "I'm going to fall in," you said.'

He blinked at her through his thickness of sleep and pulled a corner of his mouth up into a half-smile; he closed his eyes again. He remembered in his dream there had been a deep ravine, like the one in *Lionel's Journey*, and it seemed he was toppling over the edge. In the story there were people on the other side of the chasm who wanted to throw a rope across, but it was never going to be of any use. And Lionel hadn't trusted them. Why was he dreaming of that? Anyway, they had finished the Lionel story a few nights back—before he had left home. That seemed like the other side of a chasm, too. The last scene in the book had been Lionel striding down through the back pastures on his home farm, whistling to his horse in the paddock.

He drifted in a half-dream state.

Twice more he woke, looked around at the furniture in his own bedroom. The window threw an odd light over his room from the white world outside. He sank away again into oblivion. At midday, his dad helped him to get up.

'We've things to do, people to see, Christmas to be getting on with . . . ' While he bathed, brushed his teeth, and got dressed his dad paced about restlessly. He stood at the window contemplating the snow-clad garden; he sat on the end of the bed and looked at the bookshelves and the posters on the cupboard doors.

Sam ran a basin of hot water and leaned into it on his knuckles and looked at his face in the mirror. Bits of the past few hours were slipping back into memory. The clamp of his arms around his dad's neck—Dad, who had appeared among the other dark figures squatting in front of the blinding lights in the night of teeming snowflakes; then the fierce warmth of the interior of the police car; his urgent directions to the policemen to find Tony; the arrival of the ambulance just a minute behind the policemen who had clambered up into the lorry cab. The sight of Tony, in the car lights and the still-falling snow, being stowed on a stretcher into the ambulance's interior. The ride home and his failed attempt to tell his dad something about what had happened because he had broken down and cried helplessly in his exhaustion.

Sam kept an eye on his dad while he pulled on his socks, then a shirt. He went to the cupboard to find more clothes. They did not speak much, but every few moments

186

they caught each other's eye and his dad gave him the sort of smile that didn't have anything to do with words.

'Is it all right now?'

Sam stopped, one leg in the trousers, and looked at his dad.

'I mean . . . is it all right?'

'Is what, Dad?'

Derek cast about the room: the desk, the wall posters, something to help him say what he meant. He launched out anyway. 'About why you went to the motorway place. What you said in your note. It was all to do with Mum, wasn't it? You wanted to find where she was . . . Am I right? Aye, so what I'm askin' is—is it all right now? Whatever it was you needed to do, or see, or find or . . . '

This was unfamiliar territory, and Derek knew he'd made a hammy job of it. But he needed to know. Was the lad still trying to fill some Mum-shaped space in his mind? Did he still need to play talking-to-Mum games?

Sam, studying the carpet, raced back through all the hours he had spent by himself, thinking, through that day-and-a-half.

'Dad, I went back into Mum's room at St Luke's. Melanie took me. I stood in there. And I had Mum's phone in my pocket but I didn't need it any more. When I left home I thought I was going to see Mum or hear from her, or be near her or something. I didn't really know what. But I thought, Mum knows I'm coming so she must make something happen.'

'And?'

'Things happened. I had to think a lot. And, yes, it's all right now.'

Auntie Pam and Becky were in charge of Christmas dinner. Sam counted eight around the table: Dad, Becky, himself, Roy and Pam, Mrs Prythurch, and Paul and Dazz Skinner. Noisy conversations were battering and criss-crossing the table around and over his head. He couldn't really eat. He chewed a little turkey and stuffing, and he held up a crusty roast potato on his fork and nibbled the edge.

Uncle Roy was talking to Becky: ' . . . He phoned her when he was on the M6. I gather she gave him a right earful. But you've seen our Patty, though, haven't you, Becks? Behind the counter in the depot? Me and your dad go over for a coffee now and then. She's a character. Doesn't stand any nonsense from the lads. Tony must have copped it good and proper over the phone when he told her . . . '

And Paul Skinner was talking to Mrs Prythurch: ' . . . Sensitive. No, a *Sensitive*,' (tapping the side of his head), 'I'm a Sensitive. I'm clairvoyant. Some people call it being psychic. It's a gift. Always had it. I do the rounds of the Spiritualist Churches in the area. Young Darryl here comes with me.'

Mrs Prythurch stopped chewing. Then she looked down and found her bifocal glasses that rested on her blouse between the sides of her loose cardigan, hanging there from a small gold chain around her neck. She put them on and tilted her nose to focus on Paul Skinner and his son. 'Does that mean you raise the spirits of the dead?'

Skinner gave her a wry smile. 'Only if they want to come, Mrs P.' He mused for a moment, looked thoughtful, then said, 'Lavender mean anything special to you, Mrs P? Only I'm getting a special delivery from Upstairs. It's a very strong lavender scent . . . can you smell it?'

Mrs Prythurch stared at him. 'He always gave me a bottle every year at Christmas . . . '

'Yes?'

'My husband gave me lavender perfume every year. He . . . passed away on the tenth of February, ten months ago.'

'Well, no change there. I reckon you're getting it again this year, Mrs P. Special delivery.'

Mrs Prythurch put down her knife and fork and looked down at her plate. Then she looked up and gave Paul a weighted smile. 'Thank you, Mr Skinner.'

Between turkey and pudding Sam tugged his dad's sleeve. 'When can we go?'

'I'm going to phone now.'

He was back in a few minutes. 'They say come in an hour.'

There was a crowd in the kitchen. Everyone wanted to help carry dishes. At one point in the middle of it all Sam took his dad to the wall telephone and pointed to the line in Mum's handwriting. Derek stared at it.

'Eh, I can barely remember it now. He rang here and she took his mobile number. I had to ring him back about something. *Contact number*.' He shook his head slightly. Then he looked again at Sam, searching his face. What the boy had built in his mind out of that.

After lunch there were some presents to be opened.

A computer game. Shin pads, a United shirt. Three paperback novels. (One was *Lionel: The Search*) Pens. A torch keyring. Sweets.

Then Becky was called away to the phone and came back into the room with pink cheeks. Sam heard her quietly telling Auntie Pam that Constable David Shilling had rung to wish her a Happy Christmas, and to ask if she would like to go out for a drink with him on Friday evening.

Dad drove them in their own car. The snow-ploughs had been out all morning and the roads had been scraped down to the tarmac. They drove up to the entrance of the Royal Hallamshire Hospital between block walls of bulldozed snow.

There were few people about in Reception, but almost the first person they saw coming towards them was Patty LeFanu. There were prolonged hugs for Derek and for Becky; then she rested a knee on the polished stone floor. Sam looked into her damp and weary face. There were reddened bags under her eyes, with tiny creases; but she was giving him a worn-out watery smile and shaking her head.

'You know he meant well, don't you? He really didn't mean to give you all that heartache . . . '

Sam nodded. He wanted to shy away from this pained face pressing up so earnest, so close.

'He . . . he did a lot for me.'

She studied him. 'Did he? Maybe. He does have his own funny way into things. Usually the long way round.'

Derek gave a short laugh. 'Aye, the long way round, all right.'

She looked up. 'I nearly lost him, you know, Mr Bennett. That close. It makes you think about what's really important. I expect you know all about that.'

'Aye. I do.'

'I'm coming back tonight.' She waved them off wordlessly with a tissue clamped to her face. But by the time they had got to the double doors leading into the main corridor, she had run back again. 'You know what he said to me?' She held Derek in a beseeching look. 'He said if there was one thing, just one thing he wanted in life now it was to have a son like this one you've got here.'

They walked the long corridor, were overtaken by patients in wheeled beds, glimpsed Christmas trees and festoons of glittery ceiling decorations in side-wards, climbed stairs to the third floor and found Summerleaze Ward.

At the ward desk a Nursing Assistant in a green uniform directed them to a room with three beds in it. Only one was occupied. Tony lay partly raised, propped by pillows, his hair a black tangle against the white cotton. They carried chairs over to the bed and sat on either side of him. He turned his resting head from side to side to look at the three of them, and his tired smile made his eyes crease and his cheeks bulge. There was a bottle clamped to a rod above his head and a tube snaked down and disappeared under a bandage inside his forearm.

'Hey! Nobody tol' me I get visitors.' The gravel voice was half-strength; the weakened smile only reached his eyes. 'Patz been here most of the night.'

191

Sam reached out and briefly touched the stubby hairy arm.

'Tony. This is my dad and my sister.'

'Sure. I know you dad, Sam, he's my boss. Hi, Mister Bennetts. Hi, Sam sister.' He looked warily at Derek. 'Mister Bennetts . . . ' He paused, unsure how to continue. 'Is long story. Sam tell you?'

'We know the story, Tony.'

Sam watched his father's face.

Tony blinked slowly. 'You got one fine boy here, mister.' He looked down at Sam. 'Hey, Sam, you not tell me you got beautiful sister.'

Derek said, 'Tony, you did a wonderful job yesterday, bringing him back through all that. Thank you. Really, thank you.' Derek reached and gripped him briefly on the shoulder.

Tony was shaking his head gently. 'No. No. Is what I do to try put things right . . . But now I got bad news. You know what they telling to me in this place? They say is no more bacon rolls for me, no more fry breakfas'. What I do?'

Sam grinned. 'Tony? Will you bring your lorry to our house, and have breakfast with us? He can, can't he, Dad? I want him to come when Driscoll and Geordie and Dazz are there.'

'For sure I come.'

Becky said, 'It'll be fruit and muesli, Tony. That all right for you?'

Tony put a hand on his chest. 'This doctors tell me is a close thing. This heart, almost—kapooof!' He looked down at Sam. 'Why I not dead? What you do?'

'He walked off into the snow,' Derek said. 'But by then we'd had a description of the lorry from the police on the roadblock. When you didn't come and we couldn't raise you by phone, that was when I got into the police car with the officers and we went looking. We reckoned we might need an ambulance anyway by the time we found you, if you were broken down or stranded. Actually, you were out of it by the time we got to you.'

'Maybe your boy think Tony LeFanu really is messenger for Nex' Worl'. Take the message over there for real, eh? Nearly?'

They smiled. Sam looked up and saw his dad's stilled look.

Becky put some brown paper bags down on the locker beside the bed. 'These are some grapes for you, Tony. It's what you've got to eat now. To be healthy.'

He sighed. 'Is no smoking in this place. I gotta be healthy now. Is worth it? I dunno.' The skin was darkly bruised under his eyes. Something had drawn the life out of his face.

Derek said, 'Tony? Is there anyone else in your family who needs to know about you? Can we do anything? Let anybody know what's happened?'

Tony looked away out through the double doors to his room that stood wedged wide open.

'No. Patz take care of it.' He paused. 'So . . . What I do now . . . ? When I get out this place.' He looked at Sam and blinked slowly. 'I bring my lorry to you house, yes? And maybe we go for ride?'

'I want to come too,' Becky said, 'with my friends.'
'Sure.'

There was a silence. Then Sam said, 'Tony? I've told my dad about the three places you took me to, and—'

'Two. I take you at two place where you can think about you mam.'

Sam frowned. 'No. When I was out of the lorry in the snow, walking along the road . . . everything was quiet. And there was no stars or lights. And it was all dark.'

Tony's eyes rested on him, waiting.

'I was walking, and then I couldn't see the lorry's red lights any more, and there was snow everywhere, and I didn't know where I was, there was this big black silence and all the snow was lying all over me . . . '

Sam halted. Why had he started telling Tony this? Tony knew everything else that had happened on the journey home, now for some reason Sam wanted him to know the last part too. He hesitated, then he saw what it was he could tell Tony. 'You know you took me here to this hospital, and we looked up at the room where Mum was? And then we went to Saint Luke's, and I went into Mum's room? Well, I think when I was out in the snow by myself, when I couldn't walk any more . . . I think that was another place—'

Tony held up a hand. 'Sure. *Si*. But is place you only go one time in you life, OK?'

A nurse appeared in the doorway. She was wheeling a telephone on a stand.

'Mr Avenue?'

'*Si*. Is LeFanu.'

'There's a call for you.' She wheeled it to the side of the bed, then crouched and plugged a lead into the wall. 'Not too long, please. There's others wanting to use it.'

194

Tony looked at Sam while he pressed the receiver to his ear.

'Hey. Patz. Yeah . . . Yeah, they still here.' There was silence while he listened.

Sam and Derek and Becky watched him.

Suddenly he put a hand over the phone and leaned over to Sam.

'She say she love me.'

He listened. Then put his hand over the phone and leaned over again.

'She say she know what things gotta come first in the life now.'

He listened again. Then he winked and leaned over.

'She say why you tell everythings I say to the Bennetts family?'

He listened again. There was a silence. Sam looked up at Becky's face, then across to his dad.

Then Tony exploded: 'You gonna do *what*?' His eyes drifted across their faces, unseeing. He stared at the phone in his hand as if wondering how it had got there. Slowly, a smile, and then a look of wonderment spread across his face.

Derek broke the silence. 'Tony, this was a near thing for you. You'll need to take some time to get fit, to think about the future.'

'The future. Sure . . . ' He rested his head back against the pillow. '*No lo puedo creer. Ella dice que vamos a conseguirlo.*'

Then he roused himself and produced what might have been a cough or a laugh. 'You don' know what I say, eh? I tell you somethings. For long times I want to give up the lorry drivings. I want to go live in the warm, in the south, where the vines grow on the mountainside and the sun burn you face—sting! Like the smack from a woman . . . I want . . . '

Sam watched the dark eyes resting on his own face.

'I want to be the dad. And now—guesses what? Patz she got same ideas as me now—about the future.' He put his head back and stared at the ceiling. 'Is gonna happen.'

Sam got up and went to the window. White roofs. Traffic moving cautiously along scraped-out roads. Below, in the hospital grounds, a cold crow shook a pillow of snow off a tree.

'Hey, Sam,' Tony called. 'You tell me one thing, please. I bin thinking. I think about what you do. You send all this message. You leave you house to go to this Knutsford Service. Why? What is you want?'

Sam, standing between the bed and the window, conscious of the three faces watching, reached into himself. He saw the lighted passage above the road from where he had looked out into the night, and he saw the two streams of lights, red lights and white lights, drifting through the blackness. He saw his own ghost-face staring solemnly back at him in the glass. He heard his mother's voice in his bedroom doorway.

He said, 'I wanted to know if Mum could still see me in the dark.'

Rowland Molony left his Gravesend Secondary Modern school aged 15 and joined the RAF. Later in life he spent several years in Bulawayo, Zimbabwe, where he met and married Elizabeth Baxendale and where their two daughters, Emma and Susie, were born. Most of his life has been involved with poems, the natural world, the teaching of English Literature and philosophy. These days he spends time on an overgrown piece of rented land on a Devon clifftop, where he keeps bees. He has a shed there to write in, but he sits looking out of the window instead.